HENRIETTA ROSE-INNES

Shark's Egg

Kwela Books

The places and institutions mentioned in *Shark's Egg*
bear some resemblance to actual places and institutions in Cape Town.
However, this is a fictionalised account, and is not meant to be
a factual portrayal of these institutions or their operations.

Cover design by Jeremy Collins
Typography by Nazli Jacobs
Set in 11.5 on 14pt Times
Printed and bound by NBD
Drukkery Street, Goodwood, Western Cape

First edition, first printing 2000

ISBN 0-7957-0115-2

For my parents
Peter and Ann Rose-Innes

1. Motion

IT IS A STRANGE DAY TO COME WALKING BY THE SEA: cold, with grey glints on the waves, and above them a white empty sky. Her mother moves slowly, keeping her face tilted towards the horizon. They are the only people on the beach.

Joanna is fearless, tireless; she runs impatiently ahead, splashing in the shallows and talking out loud to the sea. The water is so cold it makes the bones of her feet ache. It whispers of deep-sea things: storms and shipwrecks, monsters, islands.

But Joanna is only half-listening. She is finding gifts for her mother: a dry sea-sponge as hard as a stone, but very light. A shattered jellyfish, with dense crystal flesh. And here, a curious black pod, with a spine the length of her little finger at each corner. When she picks it up it leaves a neat impression in the damp sand.

Look, look here, what's this?

Her mother turns it over carefully with her pale fingers. *It's a shark egg*, she says, her voice regretful, handing it back to the child. *Some people call them mermaid's purses.*

Joanna is incredulous. She takes the odd precious thing in both hands; it is made of something vegetable and tough, not like an egg at all.

Is it? Is it really from a shark?

She shivers with delight. A grey mist rolls in from the sea, erasing the scene.

At home, sceptical, she cuts the object open with a pair of nail-scissors. Inside, the embryo is still alive, a perfect little shark no bigger than a new tadpole. It gapes and thrashes its tail, at last expires. Her mother wraps the whole thing in toilet paper and throws it in the rubbish. Joanna is shaken, and for days feels deeply guilty.

But also powerful: she has killed a shark.

Sharks never stop swimming, her tired mother tells her; *if they do, they sink and die. It's sink or swim for sharks.*

So Joanna keeps moving – in the bath, eating her supper, even when she lies down to sleep – so that she will not sink and die. Playing alone in the big garden, she swims like a shark across the lawn, scaring up the birds. With crayons of purple and mauve she makes pictures of sharks: they have toothy jaws and enormous fins. Her mother smiles cautiously at the bright ferocious drawings.

At night sometimes, sharks swim in the dark outside Joanna's bedroom window, bumping their pale snouts against the pane. They are looking for the shark killer; they are curious. In the moonlight Joanna lies wide awake and unafraid. The silent creatures entrance her – like secrets, like the sea, like the big world waiting.

She thinks: *I am like that. They are like me.*

She thinks: *I will never stop moving.*

2. Wild animals

LEAH SAT DIRECTLY IN FRONT OF JOANNA IN CLASS. She was a book monitor, one of that misfit group permitted to skip Gym and Guidance to help in the library. Joanna was also often there, hiding from class and drawing with ballpoint pen in the margins of novels; and they were friends of a kind.

Neat and dark, Leah seldom spoke or smiled. In Maths, she would let Joanna copy work over her shoulder, moving her small hand politely aside. It was Leah's handwriting that first intrigued: her notes were written in an angular, cramped script, much like Joanna's own – not the even, rounded letters one would expect from such a girl.

She admired Leah's composure. For Joanna, the world was filled with moving light, burning and rushing ahead without her while she sat tragically at her desk, chewing and fretting at her pens, her clothes, her fingernails. The chalkboard was intolerable, the uniform chafed at her neck and thighs. She rattled the pens on her desk with her jiggling knees, laddered her stockings and smeared blue ink on her fingers. On the pages of textbooks she drew fish with sharp teeth eating other smaller fish, and cartoon heads with axes in them; "J" she wrote, for her name; and hearts, and daggers, and daggers through hearts.

To calm herself, she concentrated her gaze on the geometric precision of Leah's plait, or two plaits with a straight white parting, and wondered at how the other girl contained herself in such a world.

In the change-room before Gym, Joanna surreptitiously examined Leah's neat body, her immaculate underwear. She wore white cotton panties that came up high over a childishly flat stomach, a small unnecessary bra. *So beautiful*, thought Joanna: *her pale-brown skin, her delicate bones*. Alone at home, Joanna would undress in front of the mirror to examine her own troublesome shape: the swelling breasts, the thickening waist and hips. Her mother's cats pawed back and forth behind her in the glass, smug in their animal perfection.

From her seat at the back of the class next to the window, Joanna watched the older boys playing cricket outside in the windy sunlight. The girls all knew their names by heart; in School Assembly every morning those same names sighed through the hall in a sweet rustling undercurrent to the Lord's Prayer: *André van Eck, Brent Garson, Douglas Meyer, Robbie du Plessis* ... names like dirty kisses. Rough boys, surfers, dagga-smokers; they walked like a little army through the school, ties loose around their necks, spinning a stained tennis-ball into the air and watching the girls with derisory, hungry mouths.

They looked straight through Joanna, because she of course was a mouse, invisible; but she would pass just close enough in the corridors to breathe in their alien smell – sweat and cut grass and cigarettes. Their bodies were hard, smooth and slightly gritty, like fine sandstone; and their cheeks occasionally bloodied with little razor cuts. Not the smallest detail, not stray hair or ripped fingernail or nicotine stain escaped Joanna's meticulous gaze.

On her desk, Joanna engraved his name with the point of her compasses: ROBBIE. With religious concentration she carved the deep letters – she wanted to make them solid, something she could touch. All the girls practised similar magic: over and over they wrote boys' names on pencil-cases, in diaries, on their hands, on their thighs under their dresses; the classroom air was dense with spells. Unaware, the chosen boys were tugged and tranced with a thousand small ritual acts, with the devotional writing and recital of names. Only Leah did not indulge: her skin was unmarked, and her pink fabric pencil-case unnaturally clean, as if laundered.

At home in bed, Joanna summoned again with secret pleasure the shape of Robbie's body, drawn against the bright summer grass of the playing-field. She thought of those toys for young children, where one fits coloured shapes – circles, triangles, stars – into holes in a plastic frame. When she saw him at school, there was an almost audible click in her head – the yellow star locking with pleasing rightness into the star-shaped space – as some internal gap was satisfied.

He had long legs and white hair and a medical bracelet that gleamed like jewellery under the cuff of his white school shirt. His face was not clear to her: it was a spot of light that she could barely look at, obscured by the bleached fringe over his eyes. Sometimes she imagined putting her hand at that place on the nape of his neck where the hair was shaved, touching the short bristles with her palm; but mostly she wanted simply to watch him: *Robbie. Robbie du Plessis.* Joanna dawdled between classes, hoping for a glimpse of him down the long sunstruck corridors.

The curved bellies of the Bs were tricky, but finally it was finished: the letters even and square. Very neatly, she dotted a line of spaced points under the name. Surely, even up in the second-storey standard nine classroom, he must feel the pricking on his skin. When she put her index finger over the scored wood, it seemed to pulse with its own heartbeat.

Looking up, she was startled to meet a complicit gaze. Leah's eyes had clear, yellow-brown irises, catlike. Joanna felt a doubtful embarrassed pleasure: the name was indelible now. It had been witnessed.

Leah had placed something in the middle of her desk: a round object the size of two fists, covered in strawberry-coloured silk. It looked like a pink heart clasped in her thin brown hands. Intrigued, Joanna watched over Leah's shoulder as she pressed the little bronze catch and the thing hinged apart: in each half a circular mirror was set into pearly silk. The circles of reflection trembled, holding briefly views of the ceiling, of Leah's tan cheek, and of one amber eye. Joanna smiled back tentatively.

"Do you like it?" Leah asked without turning around.

Joanna nodded shyly. Leah turned in her desk and held the case out, carefully, as if the mirrors were pools of mercury that might spill.

"You can see both sides of your face at once," she said reverentially. "And look, it's got manicure things in it."

With the nails of her thumb and forefinger, Leah found in hidden slots behind the mirrors a file and cuticle-pusher, pulling them halfway out like miniature swords from their scabbards. Joanna, whose nails were bitten and square, was more interested in the reflected fragments of face, dress, window, sunlight.

"Do you like it?" Leah asked again.

Joanna took the opened manicure set in both hands and moved the twinned images, changing the angle between them.

"Here, look – " Leah was almost standing up in her desk in her eagerness. "Put your face next to mine."

Cautiously, Joanna glanced at the teacher; but teachers seldom watch the quiet ones at the back. She leaned forward and put her cheek next to Leah's. Together they peered into the little case, a face in each mirror.

"You and me," breathed Leah, and slowly shut the reflections on each other.

They locked together with a subdued snap of the catch. Joanna sat back in her seat, smiling uneasily. She imagined her reflection trapped inside the strawberry-silk box with Leah's, knocking up against the mirrored walls.

Leah spent much time in class buffing and filing her fingernails to pearly ovals: they were pink up until the end of the quick, then extended beyond her fingertips in perfect white half-moons.

"French manicure," Leah instructed, spreading her fingers on Joanna's desk. "Makes your fingers look longer."

Joanna nodded seriously, shoving her own clenched fists between her thighs and the wooden seat.

Leah would sometimes turn the mirrored case around, shining circles of light across the classroom onto other pupil's open books, their hands and legs. The little wandering moons stroked calves and thighs, or settled briefly on cheeks: kisses too light to be felt, messages not received.

Sometimes, Joanna would look over Leah's shoulder and see a single serious eye in the mirror, and know that she was observed.

Up on the high field a group of children stood, in the indecisive, struck manner of people at the scene of an accident or crime. From the bottom of the field, a lone teacher jogged towards them, panting in his shirtsleeves and pale blue acrylic pants. Joanna, peering over someone's shoulder, saw the body arching on the grass at the centre of the ring.

"Robbie du Plessis," whispered the girl next to her, in a slow, entranced voice.

"He's epileptic."

"They should put a pencil between his teeth," said someone else, almost drowsily; but nobody moved towards the convulsing figure.

Vehemently Robbie threw his arms and legs out from his long body and clutched them in again, preventing approach. The silver bracelet at his wrist caught the sunlight as he swung his arm. His eyes were white in his head.

The teacher reached the group and knelt beside Robbie, who at last calmed and lay still, his face ashen. He looked dead.

"Go away," said the teacher. "Give us some space here. Everybody – clear off."

13

He's dead.

For the rest of the day, Joanna sat queasily at her desk, hunched over the guilt in her stomach. She lay forward on the desk to hide his name in the wood. *Dead. He looked dead. A bad spell.*

But the next week Robbie was back at school, taller and harder, his shoulders bulky under his blazer like a man's. There was an angry length to his stride as he patrolled the school, his friends flanking him like lieutenants.

Joanna saw death behind him as he walked: a grey shadow creeping up to flick some fatal switch at the back of his head. She wanted to touch him now, hold his skull in her hands, place herself between him and danger. Because she was a shadow too, and could see things invisible to others: ghosts lounging in the corridors, darkness inside the sunlight.

She could not forget the violence of Robbie's seizure, the focused power of those rigid, flung limbs. In hard, sunlit dreams, she saw again the arched back, the hands clenching and clawing but never gaining purchase on the air. Blind eyes and bared teeth slithered and thrashed into her head, waking her up in the middle of the night, with a beating heart and a camera-flash memory – of some bright movement, some nameless disappointment.

3. The blue room

THERE WAS A SHED AT THE FAR CORNER of the school grounds, used to store wheelbarrows, hosepipes, lengths of board and wire. A narrow alley, overgrown with grass and weeds, ran between it and the perimeter fence. At one end grew an ancient pine tree, at the other a gnarled hibiscus bush, which would occasionally produce red flowers of surprising Hawaiian exuberance.

Joanna was drawn to this melancholy spot, with its remnants of a colonial garden. She would often go there to read at lunchtime, or illicitly during poorly monitored classes such as Bible Education. Sitting with her back against the trunk of the old tree, in the pine-needle mulch, she peered through the diamond gaps in the fence with fierce longing. If she crouched down low enough, she could look straight over the roofs of the houses and see Table Mountain, and imagine nothing between her and it: no buildings, no roads, no school at all.

So she sat one hot summer lunch-time. The mountain was pale, a spectral Himalaya. If she leaned forward and peered around the hibiscus into the sunlight, she could see the chestnut trees on the other side of the top playing-field. These concealed in their branches some of the older pupils, smoking cigarettes. Joanna kept an eye on the lightly shaking leaves, and was alert when Robbie dropped from them to the ground. He stood for a moment, squinting through his white fringe; then he put his hands in his pockets and strolled across the field, straight towards her.

She could only sit completely still, gripping her book. A slight movement behind her, at the other end of the alley, made her turn: Leah was looking around the corner of the shed. Her small head was extended like a lizard's on its slender neck, eyes slitted against the sun. She did not seem to see Joanna crouched in the shade.

They're coming here, Joanna realised in horror. And then: *They'll see me*.

But instead Robbie skirted around the front of the shed, and re-appeared framed in the golden mouth of the alley where Leah stood. Soundlessly, Joanna shifted in her place to watch. Leah's head disappeared. Then she reappeared in full, facing towards Joanna: her ironed school uniform reaching to just above her knees, white socks pulled up over her ankles, childish sandal shoes. Her hands were poised at her sides, back straight like a ballet dancer.

Robbie had put his back against the wall – Joanna could see only his shoulder, his right arm, a golden-furred right knee. A stray white hair from his head danced gently up and down in the sunlight: he was speaking, but too softly for Joanna to hear.

Leah seemed sceptical. She shrugged and turned her head and said a few words over her shoulder to the sky. Robbie moved his right leg forward, sliding his foot next to Leah's instep. She stopped talking and looked at him quizzically, still with her chin tilted away. He reached out his right hand and laid it on Leah's narrow hip; then slowly crept it up her waist, her torso, as her arm moved slightly outwards from her body. Then he moved his hand around to her front and stroked her small breast, rubbing his thumb roughly over it. Leah watched him with a calm, appraising stare. Then she nodded once, and stood back. Robbie's shoulder disappeared from view, and the peeled blue shed door swung open. Leah went in, then Robbie, his long-fingered hand briefly gripping the door. Just before he stepped inside, he turned his face slightly into the sun, so that

16

Joanna glimpsed for a second his bright cheek and temple. She turned her own face away as if scorched. The door closed behind them.

Joanna was down on her knees, almost touching the dank greenish earth with her nose. They had not seen her. She was invisible: she could stand up now, open the door and walk straight into the shed, and still they would not see her. *Less than a mouse, less than a bird: I am a ghost, a pair of eyes only.*

She got to her feet and walked stiffly and quickly out onto the playing-field, away from the dark shape of the shed, the bent pine, the bloody fallen hibiscus blooms. A few of the schoolchildren sitting or standing in groups on the field glanced at her curiously, then away. Joanna stood still, breathing heavily and twisting the spine of the paperback book in her hands. The shed was a nest of shadow, a clot of blood in the corner of the sunlit world. Could nobody else hear the sounds that issued from it, the moans and cries? Could they not see the ghosts, those longing wraiths that loitered on the edges of the bright field?

Leah was late for class after lunch that day. As she sat down Joanna thought she caught the sour odour of the shed: moss and rot. On one of Leah's pointy knees was the smallest smudge of earth – as telling as a wound on that unblemished skin. Joanna looked up to find Leah watching her, revealing the tips of her small teeth in a tiny amused smile. Without taking her eyes off Joanna's face, Leah delicately unzipped her pencil-case, withdrew a white handkerchief and wiped the soil from her knee. Then she raised a slim index finger, placed its tip briefly on her lips, and lowered her head to her books.

The next day, Joanna watched closely as Leah unzipped her pencil-case, turning the edge down – perhaps deliberately – to show what was written on the inside:

RduP, it said, in neatly printed letters. Underlined.

Leah thrust her hand into the bag. Joanna could not look away from those deft fingers rooting among the sharpened pencil points, the compasses, the silver scissor blades.

Joanna did not go up to the shed any more. She sat at lunch-break on the field in a circle with Jacky and Charmaine, Nicky M, Nikki K. In the sun the girls compared the shapes of their outstretched legs, rolling down their socks to show off pretty, tanned ankles. But with spy's eyes Joanna watched the shed at the top of the field, noting who went in and who came out; when Leah entered and when she emerged. And she thought: *Robbie du Plessis*. A week later: *Trevor Willis*. And then after that, in quick succession: *André van Eck, Craig Lategan, Deon James.*

And then André and Trevor. Together. And then Robbie and Trevor. Robbie, André, Mark. And more, making their way in surreptitious single file to the shed at lunch-break, like ants to spilt sugar.

Leah's pencil-case remained unmarked on the outside, but these days seemed to bulge with more than just pens. Joanna sat in class with her eyes fixed on it, affronted and fascinated by its pinkness. In front of her, Leah squared her narrow shoulders and ignored Joanna's gaze.

One day, Leah went to the bathroom during Maths, leaving her pencil-case unguarded. Joanna stared at it for a moment. Then quickly, casually, she reached a trespassing arm across the expanse of the desk and grabbed it. She sat clutching the pink thing in her lap for a moment, waiting to be challenged; but nobody was watching.

She unzipped the case and examined the interior. On the salmon lining were columns of initials, printed very neatly in fine koki pen. Some she immediately recognised, some she couldn't. There were over twenty boys in the list.

Suddenly Leah was there, grabbing the case out of her hands. Pencils and pens scattered to the floor, and people sitting in the desks around them turned to look. The two girls bent together to pick the things up, then straightened, waiting tensely in their seats until the others turned their attention away.

It was Joanna who sat forward, whispering urgently to a point at the top of Leah's neat glossy plait:

"What do you do there, in the shed?"

The plait was mute. Leah carefully zipped closed her pink bag of secrets.

"With all those boys?" persisted Joanna.

No response. Joanna remained leaning forward, examining individual hairs. Then Leah turned suddenly in her desk. She put her mouth very near Joanna's ear, and held it there for a few meaning seconds. She whispered:

"I ..."

A pause. Leah moved her mouth down to Joanna's cheek, millimetres from the skin. She smelt of warm spearmint chewing gum. Joanna kept her eyes rigidly forward, embarrassed. The boy in the desk next to hers watched them sidelong. Then Leah made a sound, low and explicit:

"Mmm ..."

It was a sample, a kiss, an invitation. Leah gave a little laugh – hot breath on Joanna's cheek – turned abruptly and sat forward in her seat again. Her shiny brown plait was segmented like an insect's body. Joanna fixed her eyes on the board, blushing and pricking the tips of her fingers with the point of her compasses.

The class went to town, to visit the Natural History Museum. It was an intolerably hot day – the sides of Lion's Head had been burning for two days, and the air hanging above the city was a crematorium brown. Joanna submerged herself with relief in the coolness of the old museum building, like a crocodile into mud.

She wandered absorbed from exhibit to exhibit: the bent, thin bodies in the San hall, eyes squeezed tight shut against the plaster that had been used to make their casts; violet crystals bristling on the inside of a split rock; a baby quagga, kept in a dark case with a timed light switch to preserve its precious ghostly stripes. In the dinosaur hall, she paused at each brightly-lit tableau to peer in at the plaster creatures: sluggish herbivores wading through a faded khaki swamp; one Karoo reptile ripping a bloody chunk from the back of another.

"Sis, man. That's disgusting," said Charmaine, walking next to her.

Irritated, Joanna lingered in the snake room, letting the others pass her by until their chatter receded. Moving in the opposite direction, she found herself on a carpeted ramp, which led up and through a doorway into a large dim amphitheatre. To one side of the entrance was an illuminated sign, black lettering against glowing blue: *Hall 4: Sea Creatures of the Southern Deep*. Hesitating, she could hear distantly the teacher's sharp admonition, the yelp of a rubber-soled shoe kicked against the floor. She moved forward into the high-ceilinged space.

Three enormous whale skeletons hung in the air. She stood for a long time with a crooked neck, imagining the dense stately bodies that had filled out the bones. Like a little child she wanted to taste them, lick at their bleached curves. Stepping back, she discovered a stairwell recessed into the wall.

She climbed upwards, and came out underwater. The room was flooded with deep aquatic light, and more creatures floated above her head: plaster models, suspended by almost invisible cords. Joanna passed cautiously beneath the jagged mouth of a shark. Beyond were two flat-bodied animals, the smaller one resting under the wing of the larger. She had seen stingrays before, but these were different, huge; if one fell it would crush her. Their bodies were broad and smooth, with delicate, rigid mouthparts and gills like knife-cuts on their pale undersides. Joanna felt a vertiginous swoon as their forms seemed to sweep over her head, the hair tugged back from her forehead by the pull of their passing. *Creatures from dreams*. Dizzily, she looked about for something solid in the room to hold onto.

There was a small breathing figure beside her in the blue light. Leah had come into the room silently, and also stood staring up at the suspended fish, mouth slightly open.

"They're beautiful," whispered Leah. "Do you know what they're called?"

"No." Joanna felt faint.

"Manta rays."

Leah was transformed by the light into a submarine being: her skin stained a soft blue, with hollows of deeper azure where her collar-bones met and under her eyes. Her voice was dulled but carrying, like sound underwater. She seemed very close, then shifting away, her image refracting through unseen planes of water. When she looked straight at Joanna, the whites of her eyes were glowing blue. Joanna took a step backwards.

"It's better by ourselves," Leah said. "Do you want to go for a cigarette? We could sneak out to town."

Joanna hesitated.

"I don't smoke."

Leah smiled, a scornful showing of blue teeth. Then she reached up and with a little jump touched the wing-tip of one of the rays, making it swing. Joanna flinched.

"I know," said Leah, slyly. "We could go to Trevor's house. He's bunking today."

The ray swayed above them gently.

"I don't know …"

"Come with." Leah's whisper was suddenly urgent. "Please."

She reached out and took Joanna's hand, startling her. Joanna did not respond: Leah's fingers felt cool and foreign and wiry. After an awkward moment, Leah released her grip.

"Robbie will be there," said Leah. "I know you like him. It'd be fun."

Something bright and tempting had swum between them in the blue dark, some prettily striped electric fish that hung before Joanna's face, in touching distance.

"We'll get into trouble," she said at last; and watched the fish dart away between her outstretched fingers, back into the dark. "Better not."

Leah's face closed down, the wide eyes abruptly lidding. She stepped away from Joanna and out from under the hanging rays.

"Okay," she said, sounding bored. "Suit yourself."

Leah did not look back as she walked away and descended the stairs, leaving Joanna alone in the deep blue chamber, circled by sharks. Joanna balled her fists in the pockets of her blazer. She felt light-headed and ill with cowardice. The ragged-tooth shark held a blind gleam in its glass eye, and the wings of the rays above her head were ghostly in the darkening room. The blue light pressed at her eyeballs and eardrums like deep water.

For the rest of the week, Joanna carried the weight of those great fish suspended over her, desolate with the knowledge of a lost opportunity – for what exactly, what unnamed excitements or communion or tremulous secrets, she could not say. The manta rays swum into her dreams that night and many nights after – passing her silently, without pause or signal, as she lay drifting in a sea as black as space.

Sitting on the field with the other girls, she felt a new scorn for Jacky, Charmaine, for Nicky and Nikki. They talked of boys, teachers, parties, crushes.

And she thought:

She fucks them. Fuck. Fucking. She fucks them in the shed. She fucks.

Turning the dirty words in her head, dark things hidden in the sunlight.

She did not have to look up to know that Leah was walking up the field; she felt Leah's movement if she were her dark twin, as if part of her walked alongside Leah, drawn relentlessly into the dim interior of the shed.

"There goes Leah," said Jacky.

22

Joanna could hear the uncertainty in her voice. *Did she know?*

"Shame, she doesn't have any friends," said Charmaine, Jacky's best friend.

"She should come sit with us at break," said Jacky.

No, they definitely don't know.

The other girls hushed as Jacky considered, eyes slitted against the sun.

"You're friends with her, aren't you, Joanna?" she continued. "You should ask her."

Joanna opened her mouth, confused by this rearrangement of alliances, wondering how she was being tested.

"I don't know her so well," she said, cagily. "She just sits by me."

But Jacky, with the moody perversity of power, persisted:

"Let's invite her to come on the weekend. We should help her to make friends."

So it was decided.

4. Kiss

NINE GIRLS HAD BEEN FAVOURED WITH INVITATIONS. Jacky's parents' holiday house was on the coast beyond Pringle Bay, an hour and a half's drive from Cape Town. On the Friday night they all went to a shabby local disco, and got lifted back at eleven in Jacky's father's Combi. They slept on the living-room floor: Jacky and Charmaine in the middle, whispering to each other intimately; more peripheral persons ranged towards the edges. Joanna was positioned between Nikki and Leah, who was next to the door. Alert to subtleties of hierarchy, Joanna turned her back and faced the warm centre.

The girls talked about the disco; about slow-dancing and French kissing.

"Did you get off with him?"

"With your tongue?"

"I like it when they kiss, like, you know, all soft and slow."

"How many boys have you kissed? Jacky?"

Joanna was quiet, pretending to sleep. She felt around her in the room the gaps of silence, the spaces where various unfavoured people lay, listening intently. Kathleen, fat but considered sweet. Sally, whose excessively frizzy hair was somehow inappropriate; of course Leah, who was here on some mystifying social probation.

"You know what, Trevor and them are in Hermanus this week-end."

"Trevor Willis?"

"Ja, and André and Robbie."

"Robbie du Plessis? Oh my *god*." A squeal from the dark.

"He had a scene with Cathy Biggs."

"Cathy *Biggs*?"

"Weird hey?"

"Anyway, Trevor said they might hitch here tomorrow."

Breathless giggles. Joanna, rigid in her sleeping-bag, felt loneliness swing open like a trapdoor beneath her. At her back was an enigmatic silence. Pretending to turn in sleep, she rolled over and opened her eyes. Leah's eyes were also open, staring. But there was no collusion there, no humour, nothing. Her gaze was patient, foreign, opaque; that of an animal biding its time among humans. Joanna felt herself shrink from a solitude even greater than her own.

One of Leah's eyes closed in a slow wink. Then she turned her face to the wall and did not move again.

Joanna lay for a long while awake, trying not to cry from loneliness, trying to imitate Leah's bleak, inviolable stare. But she was weak, and cried silently, afraid to be discovered. At last her body dissolved away entirely into the damp salty darkness, and she slept.

She was woken later by the light of the full moon through the picture window. It was brighter than it ever was in the city, so bright she could read the face of her watch – two o'clock. Joanna shifted in her sleeping bag. She was wide awake.

She lay watching the other girls for a while. Jacky's arm was draped over Charmaine's shoulder, their blonde hair spread and mingled on each other's pillows. The room was filled with stale shallow breathing, bare arms, silky hair, moist slightly open mouths. Joanna felt a sudden sharp scorn – for these soft bodies, like so many fat worms in their sleeping-bags; for their sleeping scents and exhalations, their innocuous desires. She bared her teeth at them in the darkness.

The hard light of the moon summoned her outside; wild animals were moving in that light. She got quietly out of her sleeping-bag. In her pyjamas and bare feet she slipped out of the living-room and down the passage, past the room where Jacky's parents slept, bumping softly into the second-best beach house furniture. She reached the back door and went out onto a wooden deck. It was cold outside, the air filled with the distant plunge and rush of waves against the point. Below the deck was a patch of lawn, then a gravel path edged by impenetrably dark scrub. Down to the right, she could glimpse a strip of beach, burning like a silver desert in the moonlight; beyond that, the sea.

She sat for a while on the edge of the wooden deck, leaning against the railing with her feet up in front of her, gripping her toes. She took deep cold breaths, cleaning the stale dreamed-in air out of her lungs. She liked her feet, very white against the dark wood: the small, evenly sized toes and their square toenails. With her nose between her bare knees, her arms goosebumping, she listened to the surf, vast and restless beyond the shining beach.

I could go there now, walk alone along the beach as I have been told not to do; take off my clothes and walk up to my neck into the cold cold water. My skin would be the same colour as the sand: bright silver. Silver fish would come to see what was shining. Seals and squid and sharks would swim near me, would touch my naked body with their cool skins; but I would not be afraid.

"Leah," said a voice from the dark.

Joanna nearly fell off the deck. She sat up on her haunches, gripping the railing, and stared out into the night. The voice came from the bushes that bordered the path.

He stepped onto the path, into the moonlight. *Robbie.*

"Leah," he said again.

"Hi," she whispered.

"Where's Leah?"

Robbie sat down heavily on the grass. He had a glinting bottle in one hand. Joanna stared at him, dreaming in silver and black.

26

"She's here."

He sighed.

"Come here, come sit by me."

He was talking much too loudly. She stood slowly.

"Come here."

"Shh, you'll wake them."

Robbie turned to look out towards the sea, and drank from the bottle.

"You can see the ships, look," he said. "Come sit by me, look at the ships."

Joanna hopped down from the deck and went to sit next to him on the cold grass. Robbie smelt strong and sweet. She allowed her knee to touch his. He was breathing heavily and staring out at the sea. With one hand he brushed his pale fringe aside, an oddly grace-ful gesture that made the chain around his wrist glint. She looked out into the darkness but could see nothing. When she turned back he was watching her.

"I've seen you," he said; "at school."

Joanna stared at him, speechless. She remembered his body on the grass in the sunlight, his teeth clenched, his eyes – blind like they were now, glassy with alcohol and moonlight. She wanted to hold his head, pull him bodily back from that shadowy place. *He's just drunk.* She remembered the voices in the dim room the night before – *how many boys have you kissed … you know, all soft and slow …* Leah rolling back the edge of the pencil-case, pink like the inside of a human lip, to show his name … the pale-blue door of the shed swinging open and closed …

She felt a black liquid shudder inside her, and allowed it to rise and move her forward towards him. She put her face up against his. She did not know kissing, she just wanted to feel the silver skin of his face against hers, to touch with her cheeks, her forehead … but his mouth was there, slightly open and tasting of sweet brown sherry. He pushed his face back at hers briefly with a surprised nuzzling motion, a soft click of tooth on tooth. His hand came up, icy fingertips softly on her forehead, her eyelids. She felt the bracelet against her cheek, so cold … then he pulled his head away and looked at her with sudden clarity.

"I'm going to puke," he said, and turned and crawled towards the bushes at the side of the house.

As he heaved, the back door opened and Leah stepped out onto the deck, her hair loose around her face. She stood with her arms folded, watching Robbie. When he was finished, she came briskly down the steps.

"Wipe your mouth," she said.

And Robbie wiped his mouth on his sleeve and followed her, straight past Joanna without a glance. They walked together down to the path and into the shadows.

Joanna knelt on the cold lawn, shivering in her pyjamas. She waited a long time until, in the distance on the luminous beach, she saw their linked black forms cross a patch of sand and disappear behind the dunes, out towards the point. *Straight through me*, she thought. *They never did see me.*

Suddenly too cold to think of anything else, she went back into the house and got into her sleeping-bag. She lay touching her lips with the tips of her fingers. *I kissed him*, she thought. *I kissed Robbie du Plessis*. But knew that she was a liar. It was Leah's secret, Leah's story that Joanna had tried to steal a bit of for herself. And all she got was this fake, sweet trace of alcohol on her lips; not even his real taste. It was as if he had not touched her. She tucked her hands between her legs and put her face into her pillow, hoping for different dreams.

Leah came back late the next morning, after the others had eaten breakfast. Her hair was loose and wet.

"Your hair looks nice down," said somebody. "Where've you been?"

"I went for a swim," she answered.

There was something new in her tone, something almost … *exul-*

tant, thought Joanna, watching her from the corner of the room. Leah raised her eyebrows knowingly at Joanna as she passed, and smiled. Joanna felt a jealous sickness in her stomach and looked away. She was exhausted from the night before; Leah seemed fresh and uncharacteristically cheerful.

When the others went down to the beach that morning, Joanna stayed behind with a headache. She pulled her head into the darkness of her sleeping-bag, trying to sleep. Later, she got up and sat in her pyjamas reading old Reader's Digests that she found on the bookshelf. The day was hot and windy on the other side of the picture window, and her throat was sore. On the windowsill, a porcelain dolphin leaped from a porcelain wave. Its skin was a glossy bluish white and its eyes were too small, shiny and black like crayfish eyes. Wherever she sat in the room, she could feel it smiling at her from the windowsill with those mean little eyes.

By midday she was sneezing, and Jacky's father drove her back to Cape Town. On the way he bought her a Coke and asked about her parents, and she was grateful for his dull easy adulthood. She could barely hear him with her blocked ears and nose, could barely hear her own voice answering; but it didn't really matter.

Relieved to find her mother out when she got home, Joanna went around to the back of the house and climbed into the twisted pomegranate tree. She sat in the highest branches, sniffling and sneezing like a sick child, pressing first her cheek against the bark and then her lips. The rough bark used to be too painful on the soles of her feet; but now she was older, and could climb right to the top. *I'm tougher now*, she told herself. She looked around: the garden was green, the hedge high and thick. She could hide here until Christmas, until next year.

5. Disappearing

AFTER THE HOLIDAYS, of course, they all heard the story: how Robbie du Plessis had drowned, his body washed up days later on the beach. He had been drinking; it was possible that he had had an epileptic fit while in the water. Nobody could explain why he had gone swimming in the middle of the night, in such cold weather.

People spoke about how his body looked when they found him. Jacky said he was completely white, with his eyes rolled right back in his head. But Joanna did not need to hear: she remembered his stiff, clenched body, his blind eyes. Robbie dying, on the playing-field in the sunlight in front of the whole school, and only her to see it.

If I'd put my body between them it would have made no difference, she thought. *I was less than air between them.*

Leah also did not return after the holidays. It was understood she had moved to another school in a different town. The others seemed barely to notice that she had gone: a face in the class photograph that later nobody could name. Only Joanna remembered how Leah had looked that morning when she returned to the house: her wild hair, her strange smile. But she said nothing.

She sat alone now in class, in the back corner next to the window – the traditional seat of ghosts who do not speak. She bit her lips and pinched her skin, as if the slight pain might prevent her disappearing into the air. Over and over, she wrote her own name: *Joanna Joanna*; but it looked wrong on the page. The ink was too dark, too assured to fit the body that she felt was slipping away from her, leaving her nothing but a pair of eyes.

These days, she hardly knew what she looked like – averting her gaze from any mirror or photograph, refusing the image. But despite her precautions, she would occasionally glimpse a translucent figure, reflected by a window or some other unanticipated surface. Pushing open the glass door of the art classroom, for example, she might see her pallid face swinging away in a rapid arc – a flying ghost, a trick; less substantial than breath on the pane.

She scratched bits of plaster from the wall next to her desk with the point of her compasses, staring out into the sunlight as if to blind herself. Outside, the bamboo next to the playing-fields thrashed in fury, like the necks of tall green horses riding into a storm. *Be still, be quiet*, Joanna told herself, wrapping silence around her like a skin of glass. *Shhh. Let them ride away.* She thought of Leah, her straight-backed calm, and tried to hold herself completely still.

One afternoon in the library, Joanna sat paging through the school magazine from the previous year. She almost didn't recognise Robbie in the front row of the team photo, in immaculate cricket whites, his wet fringe combed back from his forehead. He seemed much younger than she remembered – but then she was a year older now, herself. Joanna gazed at his face as if seeing it for the first time. When she tore the page out she felt a guilty sense of defiling the dead; but also the glow of secret possession.

She cut him out and stuck him down onto a piece of thick white paper. With ink and pastel crayons stolen from the art room, she worked on the picture during class, hiding it with one hand. She added shadow to the folds of his clothes and ballpoint black to his

31

grey eyes. It was a week before the image was complete: a glowing ghost-boy in white, floating above a densely worked surface of bluish black that suggested deep water. For funereal correctness she gave the picture a thick black border.

Joanna pressed the picture gently with her fingertips. Her hand came away smudged with ink; otherwise she would have put the paper against her face as well. She felt at once hungry and complete.

Then she put the picture carefully into an envelope and hid it in her locker.

Months later, she was called to the headmaster's office during one lunch-break. The secretary handed her a long brown envelope; her name was written on it in a familiar crooked hand.

"Tie your hair up, young lady," said the secretary.

Joanna, gripped by the significance of the envelope, barely looked at her. Adults were increasingly misted to her – vague figures moving at the edge of vision.

"Mm," she said absently, tugging at her messy pony-tail with one hand as she left the office.

She went up to the top field, to where the shed had stood: it had been torn down during the holidays to make space for a new tennis court. She sat down on a pile of the old bricks, careless of her dress, and examined the envelope. A Pretoria address on the back. Something small and weighty slipped from end to end of the envelope as she turned it over. She tore open the top and slid the contents into her palm: a little round mirror, reflecting the sky. The back was discoloured with glue spots where it had been pulled free from the silk of the manicure set, but the front shone. She tilted it in her palm, feeling it grow hot in the sunlight: a perfect circle of bright blue, like a piece stamped out of her hand.

"So why don't you sit with us any more?"

Joanna looked up into the milky blue gaze of a girl whose name she momentarily failed to remember. *The fat one. Kathleen.*

"Oh. I don't know. Don't feel like it."

Her eyes fell back to the mirror. Nonplussed, Kathleen stood with her arms folded across her chest, in the manner of girls who are shy about their breasts.

"What's that?" she managed.

"It's a mirror," said Joanna flatly. "It's a present from Leah."

"Oh ja, Leah." Kathleen was dubious. "What happened to her?"

"She went away."

Joanna raised the mirror and shone a circle of bright white sun at Kathleen – running it down onto her shined shoes and all the way up again into her pale eyes.

"Ow," said Kathleen, flinching. "Don't do that."

Joanna laughed and shone it in her eyes again.

"I don't think that's so funny," said Kathleen, turning on her heel and retreating across the grass to where Jacky and Charmaine, Nicky and Nikki sat discreetly observing.

Joanna guessed that she was no longer welcome into that golden circle of legs. She laughed again softly, turning the white light once into her own eyes. Then she slipped the mirror into her pocket and walked across the field alone. An after-image of the sun floated before her, black against the blue sky.

6. Sea creature

A MAN IN BLACK BATHING-TRUNKS was playing Frisbee with himself on the far side of the green dam – throwing it up at a steep angle over the water, then taking small steps to the right or left to intercept its fall. Joanna watched with interest for a moment. *Perhaps he's got nobody else to play with.* Smiling slightly, she bent again to her work, photographing stones and sticks. The mild sun lit an elemental landscape: flat water, steep shore, the orderly verticals of the pines.

Twenty now, Joanna was in her second year at art school. She had taken to dressing severely, like a Victorian widow – long dresses in blacks and browns, tight sleeves to her wrists, lace-up boots with pointy toes. She affected many heavy silver rings, less for their decorative effect than for their weight: she liked the sensation of strongly armoured hands. Her hair was very short – a number two razor – and she had lost some weight, revealing a pleasing underlying hardness: cheekbones emerged like sandbanks when the river drops. Often she inked her lips with a dark blood colour, and outlined her eyes severely in black. By such definition she hoped to contain another self – that younger, messy one, the schoolgirl who picked at her clothes and skin.

She had not lost the old habit of doodling in books, on furniture, on her hands; but her scribbles were more controlled and geometric now. She liked cubes, hexagons, interlocking triangles; complex figures, sometimes even constructed with a ruler – reminding her of those maths problems she had tried to avoid at school. For her drawing assignments she produced rigid studies of tiny hard-edged things: coins, buttons, bolts and screws. When she worked, she held her face close to the page and pressed until the pencil nib broke under her white fingertip. It was exhausting.

Joanna felt very dark next to the other students, with their summery skins and clothes. She had stayed back a year at school, and so was a little older than most of them; but the difference felt like decades. They must have found her strange – with her sombre clothes, her small pictures, her silence – and she remained largely solitary. Years later she would remember her classmates as butterflies, yellow and white, fluttering on the edges of a circle of vision. At the centre, so much more substantial, were her own two hands, dark against a pale canvas. The fingers, though heavy with the tarnished rings and often smudged, were swift and clever: they knew how to handle ink and charcoal, cameras and knives.

Her father had been a professional wedding photographer – and a drinker, her mother explained; he had died from cirrhosis before Joanna's fourth birthday. She remembered only a melancholy clouded presence, wearing a grey suit. But fifteen years later, when she found his weighty old Nikon in the bottom of a cupboard under some shoes, the feel of it in her hands had a sad familiarity, like something half-remembered from a dream. The camera was a beautiful machine, with its cold metal casing and action as solid as a gun's. She tried to keep it with her all the time.

She was using it now, kneeling at the water's edge. She liked the neat shapes of the wet pebbles, the way the sunlight made them shine like glass. As she bent forward to examine one particular stone, something splashed her face: a day-glo pink Frisbee floated on the water, still rotating. She hooked it towards her with a finger and looked up. The man had disappeared from the far bank.

35

Then suddenly he was erupting from the water, less than a body's length away, sending a small swell up the shore to wet the hem of her skirt. She rocked back on her heels, as if something had shoved her in the chest.

The stranger stood thigh-deep, frowning and dripping, and pushed the black hair away from his forehead. He was good-looking in a heavy, blunt-featured way, with narrow, bright-green eyes that seemed incongruous, like pieces of broken glass stuck into the smooth face of a statue. His body was broad and solid, and almost hairless. He made her think of an animal designed for swimming – a little clumsy on the land.

She passed him the Frisbee shyly. When he took it from her with a damp hand, she noticed that his fingernails were square and blackened, like her own. *Left-handed, though.*

"Thanks," he said, unsmiling. "Nice camera. Nikon?"

"Yes."

She held it out for him to admire the delicacy of its parts. Feeling the slope of her shoulders, the weight of her breasts, the liquid movements of her stomach, she was ashamed of her own body. So she kept herself quite still and tilted the camera left and right in the sunlight, distracting him with its gleam as one would a child or an animal with a bright thing.

She wondered how old he was. Twenty-nine, thirty. *Older.*

He tossed the Frisbee casually back to the other shore, then stood half-turned, arm extended, the muscles in his back pulled into definition. Quickly she lifted the camera and focused, hoping to steal a shot; but he glanced around in time, and grinned.

"Cheese," he said.

Joanna laughed, flustered, and took the picture. Before she could speak, he was back in the water, striking out for the other side. Carefully drying her lens, she watched as he hauled himself onto the bank and lit a cigarette. Was that a look, just a quick turn of his face towards her and away?

Abruptly she stood and climbed back up the steep bank towards

36

the hole in the fence, satisfied. She had him now, caught in the metal trap of her camera.

She loved the near bulk of the mountain behind the city, and often went alone up its slopes in the evenings after lectures, swapping her long skirts for baggy shorts. She had a favourite place, high above the city: here she could sit with her back to the big body of the mountain, and see Lion's Head and Robben Island, Cape Town spreading to the sea on her right, Camp's Bay to the left. Just before sunset, the swifts would fly in to nest in the cliffs above, black arrows shot from a luminous sky. The flock moved as one animal, turning invisible corners with the precision of a school of fish. The birds veered recklessly into the cliff-face, as if to smash their bodies into the rock; but at the last minute slipped into secret cracks, or swerved away for another sweep through the bright air.

Looking down at the sea, she would imagine great creatures out there, leviathans just beneath the surface. If they ever rose, there would be tidal waves, chaos and destruction – all of Cape Town obliterated in the flood. Only she would be saved, high up above the water with the swifts. It was not such a crazy thought: the whole of Table Mountain had once been below the level of the waves.

Not two hundred years ago, black-maned lions had hunted on the lower slopes of the mountain. Those fierce beasts were extinct now; but still it was not considered wise to walk on the mountain alone. Accidents happened. The newspapers carried reports of hikers lost in ravines, scout troops stranded on rock ledges, hypothermia and broken necks; there were stern warnings from the Mountain Club. Occasionally, one heard different stories: tourists mugged, or lone women raped in the lower stretches of Newlands Forest or above Rhodes Memorial.

Aware of these dangers, Joanna never once felt they might apply to her. Walking at dusk on the side of the mountain, she felt invisible and at home. If danger approached in human form she would surely feel the change in the air, hear a foot bend a grass stalk a hundred metres away, the insects telling. She would hide at the side of the road, or simply stand very still on the path, quiet, like a tree or stone; and danger would walk straight past her with his clumsy human tread. She would be one of a thousand pairs of eyes, in the trees and grass and in the soil; blinking, gleaming, shifting minutely to watch him pass.

There was a third kind of story, even less comfortable: unlikely people one day taking to the mountain alone, up paths they do not know, in unsuitable shoes and with no protection from the cold or rain. In the newspaper report the husband or workmate would say: *She seemed a bit depressed,* or *She had been having some trouble at work*, or *She seemed fine when I saw her that morning.* Days later, a sombre procession would carry a long plastic-wrapped bundle down to the road; or a helicopter would lift away from the mountain on a slow funeral flight.

When she considered, remotely, her own death, she imagined that the mountain might offer an acceptable end: the smells and textures as familiar as the smells of her own body, the contours reflecting the folds of her brain. She would lie down under a bush like an animal sensing death, in the sweet-smelling fynbos heat, one hand curled around a particular stone. Sometimes she could imagine nothing more peaceful. But she was sad for those other souls: lonely people from the suburbs abandoning themselves to some hard place high above friends, families, familiar things. How strange to meet death in a foreign country, in a landscape that is not your own. She thought of drowning out at sea, and shivered.

Whenever she saw the rescue helicopters above her, she would pause and squint into the sky and lay a hand on her chest, just below the throat. She was not so much crossing herself – she did not need that protection – as softly sending her heart out to whoever it was up there, lost, in pain, afraid. And especially to those who lay entirely still, in hidden crevices, in secret places; while steps away the searchers passed, calling out their names.

7. New names

S HE SAW HIM ON CAMPUS, carrying a large sheet of aluminium across the quad. The shiny rectangle concealed his head, but she recognised those fingernails. She was close enough to see her own reflection in the shivering scuffed surface of the metal as it crossed her path. Suddenly shy, she stepped into a doorway and waited for him to pass.

His name was Alan Saayman, she discovered; he had recently started work as a handyman at the art school. He stretched canvases for the students, fixed the photocopy machine, helped put up exhibits. Joanna smiled at him secretively in the corridors. Each time, she could have shouted out with the thrill of the met gaze.

She found an excuse – a broken easel – to find him in his workshop, across the parking lot behind the studios. Through the open door, she could see a black space, thrumming with the light of a welding torch. A monstrous figure in heavy gloves and mask turned towards her, holding up the torch like a futuristic weapon. He tilted the mask back from a damp scowling face.

"I'm busy."

"Oh, I'm sorry."

"Come," he said abruptly, laying down the equipment. "Inside."

39

The room smelt of petrol and paint; shelves to the ceiling were filled with tools, drill bits, electrical components whose names she did not know. There were a couple of broken-backed chairs, a pinboard, a paint-spattered kettle. Alan was moving paint cans and jars of turps off a trestle table onto the floor.

"Sit down," he said.

She sat.

"My easel," she started.

He held up a hand like a traffic cop. She waited.

"The dam!" he said at last, with that unexpected smile. "The girl at the dam. I remember."

"Yes," she smiled back in relief. "With the Frisbee."

"What's your name?"

She hesitated. She hated Joanna; the word tasted like stale bread in her mouth.

"Anna," she said. And immediately felt revealed, as if she had been caught telling a secret truth. "Anna," she repeated, more firmly.

He considered.

"You like whisky, Anna?"

"Yes," she lied again.

He brought out a bottle of Bell's from under the trestle table, unscrewed the lid and poured stiff tots into two enamel mugs.

"Down it," he instructed.

She swallowed the liquid, holding her throat rigid against the burn. He poured her another, which she held in both hands before her on the table.

"Smoke?"

"No."

"That's good."

He lit a cigarette and put his feet up on the table, right next to her hand. He wore old takkies without socks, and she could feel the heat from the skin of his bare ankle on her knuckles.

"So, Anna, all in black," he said, through smoke. "I've seen you around."

If she didn't return his smile this time, it was because her clothes demanded a certain decorum. She sat stiffly, feet together, narrow charcoal skirt to her ankles, rapidly tapping the rim of the enamel mug with the ring on her middle finger.

Her gaze avoided his face, settling on the pinboard on the wall behind him: a calendar, some photographs and drawings. She put the mug down carefully between an oily rag and a broken drill-bit – the whisky a slow heat in the back of her throat – and stood to examine the pictures. They were always easier than conversation. There was a portrait of a motorbike; a couple of Larsen cartoons; some tiny surfers on the side of a grey wave. Alan in a wetsuit, holding a crayfish. Sunset over a rocky shoreline.

"You like the sea," she remarked.

"Ja, it's the best," he said seriously. "I'd like to be … I mean, if I could I would …"

He hesitated, open-mouthed. She waited politely.

"I'd live in the water," he concluded.

"Oh, me too. I go swimming all the time."

In truth, these days she found the sea frightening. Waves distressed her: such pointless violence, so much passion spilt on the sand. But Alan seemed pleased.

"Okay, good," he said. "Then I must take you diving some time."

She smiled thinly, and pushed her mug across the table for a refill.

"Anna," she said as she walked home, slightly drunk, to her mother's house that afternoon.

It sounded good: dignified. A little Russian.

"Anna. Alan," she whispered.

New names.

Anna – no more Joanna, she decided – began to visit Alan's workshop frequently between classes. What with the whisky and the turpentine fumes, her lecturers' words seemed very remote, and she had no patience with them.

In comparison, her conversations with Alan were vivid as dreams. Leaning in close, she breathed his particular air: sweat and cigarettes, turpentine. She would watch his mouth as he spoke – running her eyes around and into that moist clever opening, catching a glimpse of the tip of the tongue, a glint of saliva on his large, even teeth. Her own tongue flicked in her mouth in a curious unison that had nothing to do with words. She imagined they were kissing secretly, standing apart, speaking to disguise the kiss from others.

Alan loved riddles, curious question-and-answer games:

If you had a tune in your head, all the time, that never went away, which tune would you choose?

If you had to be frozen at one age, forever, what age would it be?

"Nine, ten," she had answered without hesitation. "Anything before puberty."

Would you rather have no legs or no arms? One arm, one leg?

How would you die?

"Oh no."

"If you could choose."

"Not this again, Alan."

"But how? Would you drown, would you jump off a cliff?"

"I hate this game."

"Would you die from …" He clicked his fingers in the air. "From, from …"

He often lost track like this, halfway through a thought. She had to find the words to complete his sentences.

"What? Give me a clue."

He ran his hands roughly through his hair. Anna briefly admired the short vertical line that appeared between his eyebrows when he scowled – she had started to collect such little things.

"Ag fuckit, whatsitcalled, when you can't breathe?"

"Asthma? Suffocation."

"Ja, ja, suffocation!" He picked up a screwdriver and examined its tip. "Stupid word to forget."

Often his missing words seemed odd things to slip one's mind: permission, infinite, submarine. Once he forgot the word "nephew" for an entire day. Anna, who was vain about her own vocabulary, supposed he had not read very much as a child. So far she had tactfully avoided comment.

"I hate forgetting things," he said softly.

She watched him warily, waiting for more. He started to nick at the edge of the table with the tool.

"Here, I'll show you," he said, leaning forward suddenly and dipping his head. "Have a feel."

With one hand he pulled his hair forward, with the other took Anna's hand and guided it to a spot on the back of his head. There was a depression in his skull, about the size and shape of the ball of Anna's thumb. The bone felt thinner there, the skin hot to the touch, and there was a pulse – or perhaps that was the blood in her own fingers that she felt. Anna held her breath for four heartbeats, five; then gently withdrew her hand and folded it back in her lap. Her hand felt warm where it had touched his damaged skull: her skin remembering the shape of the hollow.

"What happened?"

"It was a diving accident. Hit my head on a rock."

She stared at him.

"In the *water*?"

"Yup – out like a light."

"My god. When?"

"Oh, ages ago – nine, maybe ten years. I suppose I nearly died, that time." He paused, looked at her curiously. "What? It wasn't funny!"

"I'm sorry, I know. It's just … I'm glad you didn't die."

She was grinning, and then shivering uncontrollably. The room had turned suddenly cold.

The chill of a moonlit lawn outside a beach house, years ago. The boy is in front of her, she can see his face clearly now, she is about to lean forward in the silvery light and kiss his mouth …

43

She felt a drag towards Alan as if her chair was tipping forward. She had to dig her heels into the floor to prevent herself falling upon him.

Alive, alive, she wanted to shout: altered, older, but *alive*.

"Anyway. I think I struggle with my words now, more, since the accident. It's hard to tell, really. I never was very …"

He wiggled the screwdriver in the air and looked around the room, as if hoping for something to repair.

"Articulate," she finished for him automatically.

The yellow star dropping into the star-shaped space.

He smiled, and tapped her forehead lightly with the handle of the screwdriver.

"Bang on the head. That's not such a bad way to go, hey? Quick at least."

"No!"

"So how, then? How would you choose?"

But she could only laugh and shrug. Death was far away.

8. Lighthouse

"IT LOOKS LIKE A LIGHTHOUSE," Alan had said, and she had imagined a tower out to sea, a round yellow sun, a blue wave curling like a pirate's hook.

The reality was brighter and dirtier: a narrow, tall building in one of those steep streets running up from the Muizenberg main road, painted white. When her eyes adjusted to the dimness of the entrance lobby, Anna made out mosaics on the walls: blue and gold sea horses, pocked with squares of brown gum where tiles had fallen off. In one corner, a spiral stair wound upwards; a high window was a piece of light set into the wall, too bright to look at. At her shoulder, a tiled sea horse stared with a glossy alien eye.

There was a loud rattling noise from above. A little girl, about ten years old, leaned over the railing of the stairway. Her face was tanned, oval, serious.

"Hi," said Anna tentatively.

"Hi."

The girl clattered awkwardly down the stairs, both hands on the railing. When her feet came into view, Anna saw they were strapped into roller-skates. Her dark hair was pulled into two stringy plaits, an old-fashioned style for a child. She crashed onto the lobby floor and rolled stiff-legged across the linoleum. Her eyes came level with Anna's chest.

"Is that a camera?" she asked.

"Yes." Anna took it out of the bag and removed the lens cap. "Would you like me to take a picture? Of you in your skates?"

The child looked intently at the lens. Her glance flickered over Anna's shoulder.

"No."

She skidded loudly over to the entrance, stopping herself with a thump against the glass door.

"They're blades, not skates," she said seriously, looking back.

"Oh. Sorry."

The little girl considered a moment longer, easing the door open with one shoulder, allowing a crack of sunlight to spill onto her smooth cheek.

"He's on the roof," she said, jerking her chin towards the ceiling. "You go up the fire-escape – outside."

"I see," said Anna. "Thanks."

Then the child was gone, the door crashing closed behind her. Anna stood in ringing silence. After a prudent moment she followed out into the sunlight, and circled the building to the right. At the back she found a zig-zag fire-escape, made of silver steel mesh, like a vertical cage. From habit she counted the metal treads as she ascended – *eleven steps, turn, eleven steps.* At the top, she squinted in the brightness: the rooftop was painted chalk-white, like the bottom of a dry swimming pool.

After a second, she distinguished Alan: a shadow on the surface of the sun. There was a small shed at one corner of the roof, rising above the building like the cabin of a ship; he was painting its white door even whiter.

"So bright," she complained, squinting at him. "I need shades too."

He looked around at the sound of her voice, and stood frowning, holding the flat paintbrush daggerwise in his hand. His brown overalls were rolled down to his hipbones, his smooth chest bare.

"Is it that time already?" he asked.

"Afraid so."

"Let me just put this stuff away."

Anna kept her distance as he rinsed his brush and methodically packed the paint-tins away inside the room.

"Who's the little girl?"

"What?"

"The child downstairs. She told me you were up here."

He shook his head.

"I don't know any little girl."

Alan closed the freshly painted door and padlocked it. Then he turned and came towards her, wiping his hands on the backside of his overalls. His dark glasses were impenetrably chromed, and he had not smiled at her yet.

Unclothed, his hairless torso was unnervingly broad – more muscled than she remembered it from the reservoir, quite different to the bodies of boys her own age. She almost stood aside, as one would move from the path of an oncoming car. But instead she held her ground, watching her distorted self approach in the lenses of his shades.

"Wait," she said, lifting the camera. "I want a picture."

"Jesus, do you carry that thing everywhere?"

"You know I do."

She raised the Nikon to her face like a gladiator's mask. In the small frame of her viewfinder, Alan was immediately reduced. He composed himself obediently, taking off his shades and wiping the sweat from his upper lip, leaving a tiny moustache of white paint. Eyes closed, he spread his arms to catch the sun.

Anna lowered the camera. Barely thinking, she stepped towards him and laid one hand lightly on his chest. *The flesh of some densely muscled animal: a horse, a shark.* She kissed him formally on the lips, her touch as delicate as a shadow falling across his face.

When she drew back, there was a connection, a membrane stretched between them. He smiled – at last – and touched his finger to her cheek.

47

Then he turned and walked straight off the roof.

"Alan!"

But he was floating: she could see him from the chest up, and he was laughing. She went to the edge and looked down at him. His feet were on a ledge the width of a palm, and he was stepping down further to balance precariously on a drainpipe. Behind him, storeys of empty air. He held his hands up to her, grinning, not subject to earthly gravity.

"Come," he invited.

"You've got to be kidding."

Holding casually onto the drain with one hand, he leant backwards into the void and regarded her with what seemed to be genuine puzzlement.

"No? Oh, okay … come round then. I'll open the door."

He felt with one foot for the windowsill, and swung his body down and through an open window.

Directly below, the little girl was sitting on the pavement, absorbed in something at her feet: she was checking the wheels of her roller-blades, spinning each in turn. Abruptly she stopped, and twisted around to look straight up at Anna. They stared at each other for a long expressionless moment. Then the child smiled, and just as Anna started to smile back, unsmiled abruptly, like flicking off a switch. Anna pulled her head back as if she had been spat at.

Anna found the door to number six ajar, and pushed it open onto a floorboarded passageway. She was startled by her own reflection in a mirror on the end wall – distorted, too short and squat. She wiped a smear of white paint off her face with the sleeve of her dark shirt, immediately regretting the action, and looked around: two rooms to the left; to the right, an archway leading into a living room.

Passing under the arch, Anna was distracted by flash and glitter, a sense of hot, excessive light. There were mirrors everywhere on the walls: full-length, fish-eyes, slices and planes of glass balanced above the lintels like exotic blades. Otherwise, the room was almost empty: two surfboards stood against the wall beside a battered couch; a low table carried an ashtray and a deck of cards. In the corner was a telephone on the floor. Another archway led through to a small kitchen, its walls splashed with reflection. A window held nothing but bright blue colour: half sea, half sky. There was so much light she wanted to sneeze.

It took her a moment to recognise the noise of a shower. Investigating, she discovered a pair of paint-spattered overalls lying on the kitchen floor, keeping the bathroom door ajar. She paused at the doorway, listening to the falling water.

Like jumping into a swimming-pool; like falling off a cliff.

Quickly, she took off her paint-soiled shirt, her bra, her dark skirt, her panties and her shoes.

Don't think; and then it's done.

She pushed open the door and entered the steamy chamber.

"What's your best dream?" he asked later, in bed.

Anna was feeling sleepy and pleased with herself. Sex – embarrassingly, her first – had proved absorbing, and only slightly painful. Alan's responses were a revelation: straddling him, she had been amazed by his racked back-arching, his look of driven distress. Alarmed by her own ability to provoke such sobbing climaxes, she had soothed him with small careful strokes. It felt like a shared secret: Alan's epic suffering, his difficult release.

"My best dream?" she asked, rubbing her hands. Earlier, feeling gentle, she had slipped off her rings and laid them on the windowsill. Now her fingers were unsheathed creatures robbed of their shells, banded with untanned skin. "I have a lot of good dreams."

"The best one you've ever had."

Anna was quiet for a moment. Then she said:

"There's one I've had often, since I was little. Probably the first dream I remember."

Rolling over onto her back, she clasped her hands across her stomach and frowned at the ceiling. She wanted to tell this properly, to make him understand.

"Not so much, any more. But sometimes it still comes back, or parts of it. It's about the sea."

Alan would like that; that her dream contained a piece of his beloved ocean.

"I am a young child, very small. I am walking along the top of a dark cliff next to the sea with my father. I can't see his face, but I know it's him."

As she spoke, she could not tell how much of the dream was real and how much had been invented over the years.

"I look down and the sea is dark and the waves are huge and I am afraid. But then my father says: *No, look more closely.*

"I try to look but I'm still afraid. My father says: *Look into it.*

"And suddenly there's a change; it's like those three-D pictures where you have to look through them, and suddenly you see the shapes? Suddenly the sea is lighter, more translucent, and I can see how deep it is and it's this beautiful blue, and it's full, full …"

She smiled in the dark at the ceiling.

"It's full of animals, fish and things … the colours are very intense, blues and bright greens. Some of the animals are moving so fast you can just see silver flashes, like scales or eyes. And some of them are big things that just hang there, whales, big … what are those ones with wings, they look like they're flying under water …?"

Although she knew, of course; she asked because it would please him to answer.

"Rays. Manta rays."

Softly, a thousand years away, Anna heard the whisper of a little girl in the museum, under the hanging manta ray.

"The whole sea is full of movement … and the feeling … the feeling I have is like, *Oh. I understand* … it was there all the time and I just didn't see it under the surface. Then I'm not afraid any more …"

Her voice tailed off into the dark and she lay for a while, dazzled by the jewelled vision. Alan was breathing gently next to her, and for a moment she thought he had gone to sleep. But then he spoke:

"I wish I could dream."

"What do you mean?"

"I don't really have dreams … not like that. At least I never remember them."

Anna turned to him, shocked.

"You must remember something?"

"I don't dream … coloured things. My dreams are always grey, the same grey."

To explain better, he leaned towards her on his elbow.

"They're like … stupid things. Really dull. Just grey. Like … an empty beach. A packet of razor-blades. One time I dreamed a row of medicine bottles on a shelf. Just that, nothing else. They don't move. There's no colour. There's no … nothing changes in them."

"That's horrible," she said softly.

She felt him shrug in the dark.

"Ah, not really. Just boring, you know." He tucked an arm around her waist and lay close. There was a long pause. "When I was younger, you know, before the accident … the dreams were different. I remember dreaming other things."

Anna stroked the heavy arm laid across her belly, worrying the sparse hairs between her fingers. Softly, she fitted her hand over the shallow depression at the back of his head.

"Is it sore?"

He shook his head.

"There's nothing. I don't feel anything there."

She moved her hand down slightly, away from the scar.

"I wanted to study, you know, after school," he continued. "But I didn't get in. That's why I do that shit work, at the art school. And here, fixing up the roof and painting and stuff. They keep the rent low."

"What did you want to study?" she asked cautiously, after a pause.

"Marine biology." He laughed shortly. "But maybe I'm just stupid, you know? Maybe I was always just dumb."

"Oh no, oh no," she murmured, tender and helpless.

He pushed his head back slightly against the pressure of her hand, and she dug her fingers into the roots of his hair, anchoring them there. She wondered at the foreign country inside his skull. *A grey beach. Razor-blades* – police photos from the scene of some horrific ordinary crime. Anna hated to think of him venturing alone into such a world each night.

But as long as she could touch him, track him like this with her fingers, perhaps he would be safe. Gently, she put her face near to his, so that her eyes were over his slightly open mouth, as if looking for words. His lips stirred against her lashes:

"That dream. I like it. Manta rays. That's nice."

9. Mirrors

ANNA STARTED MISSING CLASS: her lectures no longer seemed important. She spent her days on the mountain and her nights at Alan's flat. They sat up on the roof and made impossible choices: *Would you rather live in a totally blue world or a totally red one? Be too cold or too hot, forever?*

Dilemmas, transformations. Anna tried to smile: it was only a game, she knew. Beyond the edge of the roof, the sea was a heavy band: one gigantic wave suspended over the houses, poised to break.

"Come on, what animal?"

"What animal would I be?" she repeated uncomfortably. "I don't know. You tell me."

Alan was twisting a piece of silver wire absently in his fingers. He paused to think.

"Okay. You'd be a ..." he paused, open-mouthed, searching.

He made a circle with the finger and thumb of one hand and put it over his eye like a monocle.

"What?" she laughed.

"... bush-baby."

Anna smiled uncertainly.

"Why do you say that?"

"I'm probably thinking of the camera. Like a big eye." His hands twisting and twisting the thread of silver into some shape she could not discern. "But me, what about me? What am I?"

"Oh … some kind of predator," said Anna. "Something fierce."

Alan laughed, throwing back his large head. "I *eat* bush-babies."

Anna smiled distantly down at the road, the shops and houses. *There are no animals left*, she thought. *In the sea, maybe; and up on the mountain, still a few wild creatures. But here there are none. Here we are lonely.*

"I'm going to drop out of art school," she said abruptly.

She was only in third year; graduation still over a year away.

Alan shrugged his assent: "So what will you do?"

"Well," said Anna, watching his fingers shaping the wire, "I thought that I could stay here for a while. With you."

He sat quite still, seeming to ponder this.

"Okay," he said. "Get us some furniture from your mom."

With a last twist, he held the finished object out to her with a smile: a silver bush-baby, cleverly made, with a spiral tail and enormous eyes.

There was something wrong with the light coming through the steel-frame windows: it was a modern light somehow, flat and bright off the sea. Anna had grown up under Victorian high ceilings; she missed the wooden sash windows that stuck in their frames, the old floorboards with their knots and fluid streaks. There were animal faces in that wood: beaks and noses, bat-ears, dark eyelike whorls that had watched her all her life, peering from the substance of the house. In the flat she could find no faces but her own, staring seriously back from the mirrored walls.

The mirrors occupied the space aggressively, putting shine and movement into the corners of the rooms, ambushing her with unexpected planes of light. There were three in the bedroom, five in the lounge, two in the passage, three in the bathroom; one, oddly, above the sink in the kitchen, where Anna could watch herself dissolve in steam as she washed the dishes.

Small fluctuations in the quality of the glass made all the mirrors distort slightly one way or another: the tall one in the bathroom elongated, while the one facing the front door greeted Anna with her own dwarfish caricature. The big bedroom mirror was fine, except for a small flaw at head-height that gave her a spiralling eye or, depending how she positioned herself, a whorl in the forehead or cheek.

Alone in the flat, she would wander from room to room, discovering different versions of herself. In the lounge she took off her stockings, standing first on one leg and then the other, observing in the glass. In the kitchen she unbuttoned her dress, raising her hands above her head, turning her torso into the light. In the bathroom, she watched her mouth move in the shaving mirror:

Tall or short? Fat or thin? Dark or light? Solid or transparent?

It was hard to tell: she had to look and look again. Finally erasing her face with a slow exhalation.

"Why all the mirrors?" she had asked Alan once.

"They came with the flat. I could take them down."

"No, no," she had answered uncertainly, "I like them."

But occasionally, she glimpsed from the corner of her eye a woman's pale face – not her own – retreating into the mirrored distance. Superstitiously, she moved all the mirrors out of their bedroom, to have at least one place where she would not be observed. In the first few weeks after she dropped out, she spent hours lying on the double bed in the unreflective dimness, reading or looking at her old photograph albums.

The pictures were laid out like tarot cards, a reading that came out the same every time: Joanna as baby, as toddler, as small dark child. In one shot she stood in the doorway of her mother's house, nine or ten years old, a hand propped nonchalantly on the door frame. The house behind her was ambiguously shadowed, Joanna a bright, child-shaped cut-out against the dim interior. She seemed unafraid, directing a look of trusting enquiry at the camera; her only hesitation the delicious pause of a child at the edge of a pale blue swimming pool, where the water hides no sharks or wrapping tentacles.

With a fingertip, Anna touched the little luminous oval of a face. *So much more to come.*

After that picture, the sequence was broken by a blank patch of several years: teenage wilderness, a region free of images. The ghost years, schooldays, the days of terrible nervous light and disappearing body … she had destroyed the few photographs that existed of herself then. Landscapes she had also obliterated: sunlit corridors, the playing-field and the summer grass. There were no reminders of these things.

Strange that she had felt so insubstantial then; because in fact she had always been a solid girl, deeply coloured, with dark hair and skin, and eyes of muddy greeny-brown. Or so she emerged, age nineteen, on the next page of the album: a stern plumpish young woman. She would have been in first year at art school; still Joanna then, not quite Anna. In the picture she looked not straight at the camera but off to one side, preoccupied. Something had altered her expression to one of stubborn fortitude, had deflected her gaze – something that lay between the child and the woman, an unmentionable patch the thickness of a page. She appeared to be waiting, arms folded patiently across her chest, for something approaching from beyond the limits of the picture frame.

And there it came, over the page. Alan: emerging from the green water of the dam in that very first photograph. After that, there were few pictures of anybody else. With Alan, she had found her task, her project, her sole and endlessly reconfigured theme: passport and poster-sized, black-and-white, polychrome, matte and glossy, multiplied.

She kept hundreds of prints of him under the bed in cardboard boxes. Alan naked, doing a crook-legged handstand on the roof of the flat, sunlight on the smooth skin of his back and buttocks. Alan sitting astride the stomach of a sand mermaid they had built on Llandudno Beach, hands on her gritty breasts, grinning. In his workshop, sparks seeming to spout from his half-open mouth under the welding mask. A close-up of his hand with its thick fingers and black-rimmed nails, like a heavy tool laid aside on the worktable, next to the chisels and hammer. From the back, head bent, one hand pulling the hair forward to reveal the nape of his neck. The back of his left knee, with a cracked right heel propped against it. An ambiguous fold of flesh – bent elbow? Thigh brought up against the chest? An eyebrow. Toes. An area of chest just below the left breast, with the suggestion of a rib rising beneath the skin.

The images became progressively more eccentric, more oblique, more narrowly focused. She was making a map, charting every square centimetre of her chosen territory. At times frustrated with surface, she wished she could find a way inside him – through the pores of his skin, the channel of the ear, the pinhole iris – to explore internal chambers. Such dreams of penetration made her smile.

Alan was an enthusiastic model. Often she would discover him going through the boxes of prints, eagerly examining the top of his own head, his shoulder blades, the base of his spine – all the views of himself that he had been denied.

Anna unearthed her father's old photographic equipment: an enlarger, and plastic trays to hold the chemicals. Alan fixed up the windowless shed on the rooftop as a darkroom, tacking heavy black cloth over the slatted door to keep the light out. Here she would sit for hours in the bordello light of a red lightbulb, fishing for pictures in the trays with a pair of plastic tweezers. She liked it up there: the close sweet-smelling air, her own softly glowing red skin, the secretive alchemy of the chemicals. She felt hidden and safe, high above the highest tide.

Because she remained afraid of the sea. Of course it was Alan's chosen habitat, and so she had tried to understand – standing thigh-deep in the cold water, hoping to be seduced. But she couldn't bear the undertow, the drag of the sand at her ankles coaxing her further from the shore.

57

The mountain, with its gentler ebbs and flows, was a far better place – particularly on bright days, just after rainfall. Bored with flat sea vistas, Anna exulted in the uphill, fists clenched as she counted her steps – *one two three one two three one two three four!* Coming down, she ran with high, loping strides, trying to hang in the air for as long as possible. This too was how she flew in dreams: with weightless leaps, pushing herself off from the ground with every step.

Her legs became hard from exercise, her knees scored with many fine scratches. She had always scarred easily, carrying marks on her body that recorded a life of petty accident: her first bicycle collision, chickenpox, early leg-shaving experiments. Some of the scars were pale, slightly raised welts: a life story written for the fingertips, like Braille.

"Feel," she instructed in the bath, flexing her leg to bring out the shadow along the calf muscle.

She took his hand in hers to trace her scars. His forefinger paused at a fresh scratch on her inner thigh, where a thorny branch had caught the flesh.

"Look how you hurt yourself," he said. "You shouldn't go walking alone like that. Something could happen."

And Anna was wordless to explain how things were different, up there: that enormous, tiered spiderweb she had found constructed between two bushes, flies mummified in the silk. The ant-lions waiting in their fine-grained pits. The saturated blue of the sky, so blue you kept losing the specks of two hawks circling in it, the colour seeming to seep into the eyes.

It is my country, up there. I am at leisure in my own landscape. I decide where to go, and when; I turn left and right with no one's permission; I climb, I touch the rocks, I fall and stand unseen. I talk and sing to myself out loud, I lie down and rub the soil onto my hands or crush the prickly scented leaves. Nothing harms me. It is different, here in the city. Here only a few paths are permitted.

She allowed him to wash her wound. It was only distantly erotic;

but she enjoyed the slight, stinging pain his fingers caused, his intense concentration. She wanted more scratches in other places, to invite him to explore with that same devout attention her ankles, her shoulders, her back, her neck.

She found it touching: that he might think to worry about her.

10. Aquarium

ANNA GREW LANGUID WITH UNEMPLOYMENT. The money in her bank account, including a sum from her father's estate, was diminishing; but still it seemed sufficient for as much of the future as she could imagine. Time passed effortlessly. She spent the days reading, or wandering aimlessly around town: Greenmarket Square, the library, the Company Gardens.

The art gallery she knew from her student days, when she had come to make sketches. Her favourite part was the central courtyard, with its cold-drink machine and goldfish pond – each in its own way more satisfying than the artworks hung on the walls inside. She would sit at the edge of the pond, a Diet Coke balanced on its rim, and watch the orange fish circulating. When she dipped her hand in the water they came to taste her fingers.

Next to the pool were a pair of figures in bronze: Adam and Eve. They were small and slightly built, this original couple, their foreheads level with her chest when she stood up. Eve held out the apple in gentle curiosity, and Adam thoughtfully regarded it, their faces impassive and innocent. There was no sense of urgency, barely of temptation. If there was a serpent in this garden, it was a harmless beast; the Fall only mildly distressing. Anna laid a friendly hand on the top of Eve's sun-warmed head, and felt soothed.

She also visited the old museum, which had been renovated out of recognition: the hanging whale skeletons were her only point of reference. She tried to find her way back to that blue shark-filled chamber, but the narrow stairway had vanished behind a prefab partition. Exploring from the other side, she found a classroom where bones and fossils lay on tables for children to touch. She noted this with disapproval, remembering the austerity of the display cases that she had loved as a child, their contents more precious for being out of reach.

She bought a small plastic dinosaur in the museum shop – mustard yellow, with bright green eyes. Its fierce scowl reminded her of Alan's, and she smiled at the shop assistant. A friendly woman in her mid-twenties, she seemed curiously familiar: blonde hair cut in a straight bob, those pale eyelashes that gave her face a naked look …

"Jacky?"

Jacky peered back at her uncertainly.

"… Joanna?"

"Anna now – I changed my name."

Jacky had been in London; was married, had a child. She mentioned Charlene, who was a TV soap star now; and Patrick, who died in that car crash. Anna nodded, barely remembering their faces. In turn, she explained that she had been studying, was now looking for work. It sounded so reasonable that it felt like a lie. With her long black skirt, her crewcut and her fistfuls of rings, she felt both ancient and juvenile.

"And is there someone special in your life?" asked Jacky brightly.

Anna started to laugh, but controlled herself.

"I'm living with my boyfriend."

But still, she had to smile: *boyfriend*. It was probably the first time she had called him that. For her, he was never *boyfriend*, or lover, or even *Alan*. When they were together he was *you*. Otherwise he was just *him*: the other one, the one who was not her.

"No wedding bells, then?"

"Oh god, no."

In her head, Anna was starting to feel the presence of a school-girl with a dirty dress, sulking and sneering. She ignored her, as one should a naughty child. But unable to leave the past altogether alone, she had to ask:

"There used to be a room here, long ago, with sharks in it? Models, hanging from the roof?"

Jacky shook her head doubtfully.

"No. Before my time, I'm afraid. They've changed everything around. But you know, you should try the aquarium. They've got real sharks there. It's nice for the kids."

As Anna walked back through the formal gardens in the sun-light, past people eating their lunch on the grass between the statues of horses and naked men, she glowed with the pleasure of this or-dinary exchange. She felt heavy pieces of childhood sloughing off her like glacial ice melting. *Was I wrong?* she wondered, examin-ing her school memories, so filled with longing and dread. That all seemed so far-fetched now, so distant and unlikely.

Have I misremembered? All that terrible light, the fraught lone-liness – was it in my head? Were we all just nice little girls?

Anna had always been susceptible to superstition. When, soon af-ter her conversation with Jacky, she saw the tiny ad in the classi-fieds, she recognised it as a certain sign. The aquarium needed a photographer for their in-house magazine, *Aqua*. A laughably small salary; to start at once.

Ambushing herself with a burst of efficiency, she typed up a CV on her mother's antique typewriter. It did not take long: she could only fill two sparse pages.

Grimly she took stock in the bathroom mirror: her hair stuck up at odd angles, there was a pimple on the side of her nose, and her clothes were from the Salvation Army shop. She ran a hand through her hair, considered lipstick; lightly head-butted her own cold glass forehead.

Fuckit, she thought. Defiantly she folded the CV in four and put it in her pocket.

She arrived an hour and a half early for the interview, and bought a ticket at the front like an ordinary visitor. Inside, the aquarium was dimly lit, and carpeted with something thick and springy underfoot, like the stomach of Jonah's whale. Over the PA system, whales sang their sad, foreign music.

The tanks glowed blue in the dark, fish turning and coursing on all sides. Anna put a black hand against the side of a tank of rushing pilchards. To these creatures she must seem like a wraith tapping on the glass sides of the universe; a ghost from the world of air. She shivered, feeling unreal and shadowy.

Living things, she thought with awe, *with blood and heartbeats and eyes that open and close, down there in the deep cold ...*

It was the predator tank that drew her, the big green jewel at the heart of the building. Here, two ragged-tooth sharks swam around the central rock, their heads bleak masks. It was a few moments before the great opalescent ray came winging past, its body pale in the shaft of sunlight from a skylight.

Anna felt her ugly mood dissolve. She sat quietly in the amphitheatre facing the tank, watching the stately passage of the ray and the slate-coloured sharks that flanked it. The animals coursed at different speeds, completing their circuits in some slightly off-kilter synchronisation: a complex cycle of slow rhythms that she could not follow, the winged ray in counterpoint to the sharks. After sitting for twenty minutes she came to anticipate the rare moments when all three came past together.

Between her and the animals, people were fractious shadows, too blurred and rapid to be real. Occasionally someone would take a photo, the flash bouncing back off the glass. The sharks swam on oblivious, their motion relentless and perpetual.

Hugging her bag to her chest, she felt the hard weight of the camera inside it. There were so many pictures to take here: not just of the animals, but of this whole split world – the tanks lit up like TVs; the dim human creatures pressing against them, unable to penetrate. Her own reflection in the glass: flesh rendered translucent, insubstantial.

She touched the folded CV in her pocket, and felt a giddy, mixed pang – both anxiety and elation.

The job is mine. It has to be.

11. Calm

THEY GAVE HER AN OFFICE TO HERSELF. On the first day, as soon as she was alone, Anna bolted the door, sat down in the swivel chair and took stock. *This computer, this filing cabinet, that small fish-tank in the corner – all mine, now.* In each of the six desk drawers was pristine stationery: unopened boxes of staples, an eraser still in its plastic sheath, drawing pins with smooth plastic heads. Everything was modern and correct, soothing in neutral shades of grey and cream, and very clean.

She examined the laminated poster behind the desk. A dozen sharks were arranged against a turquoise sea: *Whale Shark. Ragged-tooth Shark. Hammerhead. Great White.* Next to the poster was a grainy black-and-white photograph of a delicate perforated sphere, like a seed or the skeleton of an odd limbless animal, suspended in grey plasma. When she closed her eyes the image turned in her head. She wondered how big the object was in reality: probably invisibly tiny, impossible to pick up on the most careful fingertip. One would know the presence of such beings only when massed in their millions – a tint in the swell at a certain angle to the sun.

Anna became aware of a light mellifluous bubbling coming from the corner. With a kick against the desk, she rolled the chair over to have a closer look. She had thought the fish-tank was empty,

65

but now she saw, pressed into a crevice in a rock, a small, rust-coloured octopus. Its eyes were closed to pearly slits, and it pumped water in and out of a valve with a snoring motion. She tapped her fingers against the side of the tank. Smoothly, a tentacle roped out to touch the place on the glass with an inquisitive tip.

She remembered a day the previous summer, walking on the rocks with Alan. He had squatted at the edge of a tidal pool to point out a stranded baby octopus.

"Know how you kill it?" he had asked.

"No?"

"You turn it inside out like a glove, and then you smack its head on a rock."

Vigorously miming the action, he had nearly toppled into the water. She had stared at him, appalled.

"That's awful."

"It's very quick."

Frowning at the memory, Anna experimentally dipped her hand into the tank to touch the creature's skin. It considered, then wrapped the tip of a tentacle around her finger; and seemed to blush, just slightly, a deeper rose. She bit her lip in pleasure. After a moment, she carefully withdrew her hand and wiped it on the leg of her pants.

She paced out the room: three big strides by four across. Finally, she lay down on her back on the fawn carpet, and breathed in the deodorised grown-up smell of it all. No marks on the walls, she noticed with awe; not one scribble or scuff, no evidence of despair. Hard to believe, that she might inhabit such a peaceful place.

That sense of peace did not desert her. Every morning she felt it enter her body as she stepped up off the Muizenburg platform, the train doors sucking closed behind her. As the train gathered speed, the leaping springbok engraved on the window floated over the fleeing suburbs – shivering as the train changed tracks, staying with her all the way to town.

The aquarium was right on the waterfront. At lunchtime she would sit on the pier and converse with the gulls, admiring the big bull seals that hauled themselves onto the tyres roped against the harbour wall. She was not afraid of the sea here: it was tame.

Sometimes she would window-shop, dawdling in the marbled walkways of the mall, feeling dusty and pagan in her clothes of black and bloody purple. A childish part of her loved the pricey fakeness of it all – sweet and unnecessary, like ice-cream. It made her feel young – seventeen years old, silly and light as she had never actually been at that age. She was sixteen, fourteen, twelve. She bought silky underwear to wear, secretly, under her old black clothes; pearlescent lotions, skin creams like melting butter. Curios, souvenirs from the country of girlishness.

They celebrated her birthday on the rooftop with a bottle of pink champagne. Alan's gift was a bright blue dress with a short skirt. Two years before she would have scorned such frippery; but now she immediately stepped out of her old clothes, right there on the rooftop, and slipped on the new dress. Mesmerised, she spun the skirt around her thighs. Against the white paint of the rooftop the fabric glowed, seeming to leave a blur of colour behind her when she moved. She felt she could jump straight off the roof and fly.

"Sexy thing," said Alan; but his voice was shy.

Anna smiled at him uncertainly. She would have to practise this, this being young.

As summer approached and the afternoons lengthened and slowed, Anna's body forgot its old twitchy restlessness – the jiggling knees, the doodling, the fretting at the substance of the world. Unchewed, her fingernails grew slowly longer: every week she would cut their little half-moon rinds and lay them out in order on the top of her computer hard-drive, marvelling. Her mother had always told her it was dangerous to leave hair or nails lying around – witches might use them to lay spells on you. So Anna counted the clippings carefully before carrying them in her palm to the staff toilet to flush away. On the way back to her office, she would pause in the trapezium of amber light cast down from an undusted skylight, turning her face towards it like the head of a sunflower.

If you had to be frozen at one age forever, what age would you choose?

This age, she thought, the sunlight pale red through her eyelids. *This age, now, right now.*

Anna's job description expanded: she built displays, designed T-shirts, wrote brochures, and took school groups around the aquarium. This last task was surprisingly satisfying. She would imagine herself a priestess, escorting pilgrims into the presence of monstrous deities: sharks, giant crabs, the rare sunfish. After exactly twenty-seven minutes, she led the children safely out again, to air and cooldrinks and other earthly pleasures.

She worked hard on her schools lecture: *Sea Creatures of the Southern Deep,* she entitled it, vaguely recalling the phrase from somewhere. It was delivered in a voice that felt quite unlike her own: resonant, earnest, with a hint of urgency. Her message was complex. Mating seasons, diet, endangered status – these were all important, surely; but she also tried to convey more personal information:

Look, the curve of the seal's back; the brief jewel of the little fish; those long black-and-white-striped poison spines, how they sway, so elegant.

Look, pictures, shapes.

See how many fierce and lovely things there are, out in the big world. Children, take heart.

She thought often of Alan's frustration with words during these tours. Because on the whole her speeches were ineffectual: the children gave her back hard eyes like marbles, or ignored her completely. Once, while explaining external fertilisation, Anna watched from the corner of her eye a girl breathe onto the cool glass of the shark tank, and draw a heart in the mist with her pinkie. At that

68

moment the great mask of a shark loomed beside her; but the girl, turning to giggle with a friend, did not see it slide past.

The children seemed very young to her, and all so pretty. Skins were impossibly tender, eyes without pain; soft, newborn things that would shiver and melt if you touched them. She did not remember such lovely frailty from her own schooldays, although she supposed the children were much the same – except, of course, her classmates then had all been white. She bestowed particular smiles on certain individuals: stocky Joannas, slender-wristed Leahs, in different colours.

Sometimes, a sulky Robbie would glare at her, hands in his pockets. Anna would note the pierced ear (earring removed for school), the cigarette-pack bulge in the back pocket, the odd socks – and be entirely charmed by such details. Boys like that fascinated her, with their raw new bodies, their big hands and loud mock-toughness. Always, they asked about the sharks:

Miss, can that one eat you?

Miss, did anyone fall in the tank ever?

They really loved the sharks, those boys.

Going home in the evenings, the train trip seemed a long and perilous journey. As she approached Muizenberg, Anna could feel the layers of atmosphere thickening above her, descending, loaded with spray and darkness. In places, when the sea was rough, the water washed over the tracks and smacked up against the windows of the train, startling unwary passengers with its violence.

At home, Alan waited: a secret pleasure, an unopened gift, a wild bird locked in her bedroom. Pacing the corridors of the aquarium, placing her feet carefully inside the lines on the carpet, she thought about him; turning his body in her head, examining him from different angles.

He was working less frequently now – going in to the art school only two or three times a week, home early in the afternoons. She could not imagine what he did in the flat all day: he had few friends, there was no TV and he didn't read. Of course she knew he did odd jobs around the building, and surfed, and swam; but she could not picture it. In her mind's eye he was always quite still. She saw him balanced on the very edge of the roof, arms outstretched, frozen. Or standing entranced in the mirrored lounge, watching his reflection recede forever. Only when her hand turned the front door key in the lock could he wake from his charmed sleep, move and speak again.

She worried, vaguely, that he would lose his job; or that he had lost it already and not told her. But a secret, flawed part of her quite liked the idea of keeping him at home: close at hand, hidden from other people. Particularly from all those little girls at art school: she had seen them slipping their eyes at him, the handyman with his heavy good looks and his dirty fingernails.

Because she did most of her photographic work at the aquarium now, Anna sold her developing equipment. The black cloth came adrift from the door of the darkroom and was bundled away in a corner; but the red light-bulb stayed, adding drama to the piles of junk and tools that slowly filled the space.

They spoke, awkwardly, of getting a housemate for the third room, to help with rent. Then retreated quickly from the idea and did not discuss it again. The thought made Anna feel slightly sick. Solitude – which Alan did not compromise – was a habit she had found early in life, and was unwilling to abandon now.

She really knew no one besides him. Sometimes she wondered how this isolation had come about; when, exactly, she had lost the ability to be a person among others. Occasionally – window-shopping, or taking her solitary lunch on a bench beside the water on a clear day – she felt an absence at her side, a space where someone else should be. Perhaps a girl of her own age, to whom she might casually turn with a laugh – to remark on the weather, the passing tourists, on this or that. Whatever people spoke about.

Sometimes, even now, she dreamt of Leah.

There was one dream, particularly, that came again and again.

In it, she was in her usual place on the mountain, looking down on the city. But the tide had come in, and Cape Town was obscured by a sea of silvery mist that she knew was the ocean risen, coming to just below her feet. Robben Island was under the water, even Lion's Head overwhelmed. There were seagulls circling high above her head in the white air, but otherwise no movement except for sparkling trails of vapour rising and subsiding.

Then they appeared: Leah doing slow somersaults out over the edge of the cliff, and Robbie, smiling and paddling near, beckoning her to join them. With dream strength, she reached out and grabbed his hand and pulled him out of the mist, which was chill like vaporous ice. She held her body against his cold one, and felt him thawing next to her skin.

But Leah did not smile or wave or draw near. She looked at them as a seal might glance from the surf at fishermen on the quay: with animal scorn. Before turning and plunging away into the luminous element, into bright inhuman realms.

Waking from this dream, Anna would feel quite hollowed out with loneliness; even though Alan slept next to her, skin to skin.

But those moments were rare. In bed in the brazen mornings, yellow sunlight on her skin, Anna lay amazed at her own joy: at her body's exposure, at Alan's gaze on her. At being seen.

Most of the time, it was enough.

12. Ghosts

SOMETIMES GHOSTS RETURN, years later, and walk straight into your house, as if they had never left.

Anna should have known. She should have felt Leah's approach in the change of weather, in the rise of the berg wind. This was the weather she remembered from school, as if it had been like that all the time: a hot brightness in the air, blue dazzle off the choppy swimming-pool. Boys uncomfortable in their blazers and ties, girls holding down their skirts with outstretched fingers, faces concealed by veils of hair. Restless weather, when you can't put your mind to anything.

And coming in on that hot wind was a small figure in a pale-blue schooldress, holding a little mirror in the palm of one hand, reflecting lost sunlight into Anna's eyes. Coming back through the years, dead chestnut leaves blowing around her feet.

Berg wind weather; weather for ghosts.

At first there were just hints: teases, footprints in sand, shadows walking. One grey evening as Anna came out of the aquarium, she glimpsed a narrow body moving quickly sideways between the people on the opposite pavement. Not immediately human, the figure resolved into that of a woman wearing tight dark clothes – skinny jeans, a dark jersey, a grey knitted hat that hid her hair. There was nothing definite to tug the cord of recognition that ran up Anna's spine into the back of her skull, so hard that she felt her chin jerk up; just the way the woman looked briefly over her shoulder, a certain rapid precision in her steps. Then she was gone, descending into the mouth of the underground parking lot. Anna stared, as if expecting something to rise from the dark portals in a cloud of smoke like a pantomime devil.

It wasn't, Anna told herself; *it couldn't have been.*

The next time was on Camps Bay beach, at midday on a bright Sunday. Anna sat masked in sunscreen on a black beach-towel. Alan always laughed at that towel – *goth beachwear.* She scanned the surf, spotting him at last far down the beach, talking to a girl in a blue swimsuit with long dark hair down her back. She was as small as a child: Alan had to bow his thick neck to bring his head down to her level, like a horse or bull pawing the ground. The girl stood very straight, her small breasts pushed outwards in answer to his chin's thrust, hands at her sides and her own chin tilted upwards.

Anna almost expected Alan to raise his arm and run a hand heavily up the girl's swimsuited side. But the stranger took a step backwards and with a flick of her hair walked away; and Anna could see she was different: too young, perhaps a bit plump, the hair too thick.

He was only flirting with some girl, she thought, and laughed at her own relief. She wanted to go to him, wrap him in the towel like a wandering child and take him home, away from the sea and its pretty ghosts.

Neither of the women she had seen was Leah; but each time she acknowledged that her relief was tainted with something else, something strangely like disappointment. When she turned these incidents over in her mind they had an alien feel and weight, like stones from another planet. She fretted at their ambiguous shapes, fitting them together in different ways. They had a certain taste of truth, or prophecy.

That Monday morning Anna sat sketching in front of the tall kelp-garden tank, her eyes filled with its tan and green luminous sway. Looking into the water, she let her eyes unfocus, flattening into one plane the hypnotic movement, the fish hanging between the pale green-brown fronds.

And there, suspended between the glossy slender columns of kelp, was a human figure, a flat, smudged shadow of a child under water. Anna's drawing pad fell to the floor. Startled, the shadow figure retreated backwards into silky greens and browns. It was the refracted image of a person looking into the tank from the other side, Anna realised: a trick of the light. She wondered if it was a straggler from the school group that had come through earlier.

The person pressed four fingertips to the glass, and then moved, trailing a hand against the luminous tank. Anna watched those precise pink pads sliding, and waited. When the woman emerged around the corner of the tank, she was reduced, small and clear and close. She leaned against the side of the tank, one hand flat against the greenly glowing glass. On the other side of the glass, little fish seemed to constellate around her head like a sensitive halo. A large flat-sided fish with yellow lips briefly mouthed the place on the glass where the stranger pressed. She pulled her hand away and examined it, as if expecting the glow of the tank to have come off on her skin like phosphorescence. The big fish sombrely back-paddled, paused, and moved on. *Those fish never did notice me,* thought Anna, *even though I banged the glass.*

Hidden in the relative darkness, Anna examined the woman carefully. She was small, with spiky, whitish hair, and was wearing something that looked like a pair of pale pyjamas. Carefully, Anna picked up her drawing pad. The woman glanced up at the sound, noticing Anna for the first time. She came closer and peered at the pad on Anna's knees.

"How do you see in the dark?" she asked.

The voice was conversational, bold. Most people whispered in the aquarium, as if in the presence of religion.

"The eyes adjust," Anna answered, resisting the impulse to cover her drawings with her hand.

The left side of the stranger's face was green-lit, the other half in darkness. It occurred to Anna that she must be similarly masked. Alongside them, silver shapes hung silently, watching the stranger with fishy covetousness. The kelp waved, as if subtly trying to catch her eye.

"You're good," the stranger remarked.

"Thanks."

"But then, you always were the artist."

A bubbling silence. The woman turned her face slightly, and her eyes caught alight, irises gleaming a fierce impossible gold. Anna felt recognition like a soft blow to the back of her skull.

"That's not your name," the woman said, touching the name-tag on Anna's chest.

"I changed it," Anna said at last.

"Ah," said Leah. "I've changed a little too."

13. Lucky fish

"I'VE NEVER BEEN HERE BEFORE," said Leah. "It's nice."
They sat at an outside table at the Gardens Tearoom. An enormous gum tree leaned over them, its smooth white branches like human limbs – bent elbows and knees, skin wrinkling where the branches joined the trunk.

Anna was staring. She was in the presence of some creature not quite human: Leah seemed to be contained in a soft glow, casting a pale light onto the polished knives and forks. She wore a loose shirt and trousers of yellow silk. When she turned her head slightly to the right, a star-shaped nose-stud caught a speck of light. Her skin was still tan and smooth – but paler than Anna remembered it, as if dusted with some translucent powder, and drawn a little too tight across the bones of the face. Her short hair was bleached white and gelled into tiny points, except for a few long strands that grew from her temples like delicate sideburns. Only the skin on the backs of her hands showed any signs of ageing: it was finely tessellated, like the skin of a lizard.

But it was the eyes that demanded attention: they were a moist and radiant gold, an unnatural colour, like wet metallic paint. Not human at all.

"My mother used to bring me here, when I was little," Anna

said, remembering some indistinct, summery part of her child-hood that predated school. "There used to be these cats here, living in the bushes. They ate the leftovers."

"What sort of cats?" Leah was interested, serious.

"Grey and white, tabbies. Must have been somebody's pets, once. They had kittens in the flower-beds."

Leah turned expectantly towards the shrubbery.

"Where?"

"Oh, I don't know what happened to them," answered Anna, inadequately. There was a moment's silence. "You know, I didn't recognise you at all," she said. "With the hair, and everything."

"Short's the best, isn't it?"

"And your eyes," Anna said, touching her own eyelid. "Are they …?"

"Fake, yes. Coloured contact lenses. Do you think they're creepy?"

"No, I really like them. Striking."

"But you – you look just the same," Leah said.

Anna laughed shortly, offended.

"I was hoping I'd changed a bit."

"No, no, you really haven't."

Anna bent to push a folded paper napkin under one leg of the unsteady table. She found herself abruptly eye to startled eye with a pigeon looking for crumbs.

"Hello, you pigeon," she said softly, feeling about eight years old.

Leah's feet were side-by-side under the table, positioned as neatly as shoes beneath a bed. They were bound into thin-strapped golden sandals, toenails painted to match. Anna elevated herself carefully above the table again, to find Leah watching her closely.

"I saw you on TV," said Leah.

"No, really?" Anna was intrigued.

"There was this thing on the aquarium – a kid's show. You were in the background."

77

"I remember when they came to shoot that. I didn't think I got in."

"Just for a second. But I recognised you straight away," said Leah. "That's how I knew where to find you."

"Oh, right."

There was a pause while the tea arrived.

"So – why did you come back to Cape Town?" Anna asked, when the waitress had gone.

"What do you mean? I never went away."

"But I thought – after you left school, didn't you go to Pretoria, or somewhere?"

Leah made a face.

"Oh that ... that was just for a while," she said vaguely. "No, I live in Cape Town. I've been here all along."

"Doing what?"

Leah laughed shortly, and placed the fingertips of both hands against the curve of the teapot. The nails were still perfect ovals, but varnished now in pale metallic gold, the same as her toes.

"Not doing much. I'm unemployed. Staying with my boyfriend in town. He's a musician."

"In a band?"

"Classical. He plays the oboe."

"That's nice," Anna said politely, trying to picture an oboe.

Leah's fingernails rapped impatiently against the porcelain.

"Actually it's crap. I need to find another place. And I really need a job." She put her hands in her lap, and smiled brightly at Anna. "But look at you. You've done alright."

"Have I?"

"Of course. You're an artist – you lucky fish."

Anna laughed. The silly slang was incongruous – something from childhood, earlier than high school even.

"I wouldn't call myself an artist. I take photos, mostly."

"That's art. You always were good at that stuff, at school. Drawing. You were famous for it."

Anna looked up sharply.

"I wasn't famous for anything in high school," she said.

"Yes, you were. Everyone thought you were good. I was so jealous."

Anna searched Leah's face, but could find no signs of mockery.

"How could you possibly have been jealous of me?" she asked softly, amazed.

Leah didn't answer. In the silence, her hands were arranging the things on the table: straightening the salt cellar, touching the knife and fork into position. She picked up the knife and reflected the sunlight off its blade onto the tablecloth, a slight, tense smile on her face.

"Do you think about school, ever?" Leah asked eventually.

"I try not to."

"It was shitty, wasn't it? The worst time."

"Completely. Do you remember ..." Anna hesitated; but she couldn't bring herself to ask about the drowned boy, not yet. "Do you remember Maths class?"

Leah shook her head slowly.

"I don't remember much, from then. Except for you. I remember we were friends." A quick, radiant smile. "Best friends."

Anna felt a strange, embarrassed pleasure. She was terribly unused to these things, these rites of friendship.

"Yes," she said softly, smiling down at Leah's neat, restless fingertips. "Yes. I suppose we were."

Out of the corner of her eye, she glimpsed a grey cat darting into the bushes. But she kept very still, not turning her head to see the ghosts at play.

Later, she sat in her office watching the screensaver – sharks ceaselessly turning, gliding, turning through violet seas – and remembered the conversation, word for word.

Maybe it really was like that, at school. Perhaps I have been mistaken. Perhaps we were all just nice little girls.

Lucky fish, best friends.

Such potent words; even now.

Anna frowned at herself in the mirror at the foot of the bath. Through the wall, she could hear Alan's familiar clatter: washing the supper plates, clearing his throat. There were puzzling pauses, in which Anna could sense him breathing. An impatient percussive tapping: a knife handle rapped against the aluminium sink. *Alan is thinking.* Now a slow, pensive scouring – cleaning the frying pan perhaps – the sound suggesting a worried, circular train of thought.

A heavy tread down the passage. He came into the bathroom, sat on the edge of the bath and put his fingers into the hot water at her feet. He gripped Anna's big toe.

"Ow, let go."

Alan moved his heavy hold up her foot, sliding his hand around the heel, up the ankle and the calf, backward against the short growth of hair on her leg.

"So, this person," he began.

He lifted his hand out of the water and watched the soapy drops gather on his fingertips.

"Leah."

"Leah. What's her story?"

"I told you. Her boyfriend kicked her out. She doesn't have a place to go."

He was dribbling water from his fingers onto her breasts.

"And this would be for how long?"

"A few weeks. Say a month. Two max."

He moved his hand through the air and hung it above Anna's face, dripping milky water in her eyes. She pushed his hand away.

"When would she come?"

"Soon. As soon as you say it's okay."

Alan stood and ran wet fingers through his hair, catching his reflection sidelong in the mirror.

"So is she cute?"

This was a joke, of course. Anna considered.

"Not cute. She's beautiful."

He flicked drops off the tips of his fingers onto the bathroom floor, smiled.

"Well. That's decided, then."

Leah pulled up outside the flat in an old blue Mazda. Going down to greet her, Anna saw that she had changed from gold to black. She wore a black T-shirt with a high neck, and tight black leggings through which Anna could see the knobs of her hipbones. The nosestud was gone, and the flimsy sandals had been replaced by thick-soled black boots. Her nails were enamel black, and her hair, impossibly, hung in multiple thin black braids to her shoulders. Over her shoulder she carried a satchel of shiny black leather, in one hand an olive-green suitcase. Her eyes looked hard and brassy.

"My god, I didn't recognise you," said Anna. "Again."

Leah seemed possessed of a curious playfulness:

"Wig," she said, tugging at a braid. "Look, we match." She stood up close to Anna, cocking her hip against Anna's softer side. "Black on black. Such goths."

Anna moved uncomfortably away from the bony pressure. She felt mocked.

"Is that all your stuff?" she asked.

Leah hefted the suitcase and nodded.

"I never bring very much with me," she said. "But I steal the towels when I leave."

"Ha ha," said Anna, feeling a sudden tenderness towards her towels – new ones, in a beautiful deep purple. "Here. I'll take the suitcase."

In the lobby, she caught sight of their reflections in the glass door. They did indeed match each other: dark twins, the body and its shadow.

As Leah slipped quickly past her into the flat, Anna had a sudden cold sensation that she had made a mistake, done something irreversible. As if she had opened a box and released something dark and cold and lithe. She followed, closing the door behind her.

Leah stood in the centre of the mirrored living room, looking around with hungry eyes. Gripping her satchel, she looked like a refugee from some disaster where hair and clothes and possessions have all been charred completely black. She closed her fake eyes in a slow blink, and then turned them on Anna in the doorway.

"And my room?"

"Through here," said Anna. "We put in some furniture for you."

Alan had found a single bed in the garage, and they had actually bought a second-hand wardrobe. Anna had put up some posters filched from the aquarium: dolphins and tropical fish.

"It's small, but it's nice and sunny in the mornings," Anna continued.

Turning, she found herself speaking to an empty room. She put the green suitcase down and went through to the lounge. The back doorway onto the fire-escape was open. Walking out onto the metal-mesh landing, she saw nothing below her; but above, on the next turn of the fire-escape, the black satchel sat abandoned. She climbed past it.

It was Leah she saw first, standing at the very edge of the roof. She seemed unaware of the drop behind her, flexing her back lazily and rolling her shoulders as if they were stiff. Her eyes were meditatively fixed ahead of her. Anna followed her gaze.

It had become Alan's habit to sunbathe on the roof: he was laid out on his back in the exact centre of the white concrete space, naked but for his shades. His arms were straight at his sides: a toppled statue. Sweat glistened at his temples and on his upper lip; Anna could almost see steam rising from his flesh.

"Who's that?" asked Leah, pointing with her chin.

"That's Alan," said Anna, embarrassed.

The two women stood silently for a moment, regarding the naked man. Alan lay entirely still, refusing to open his eyes. Anna started to giggle.

"Aha," said Leah. "Nice, very nice."

She put her hand to her face and crooked her index finger, taking the picture with a camera made of air:

"*Click.*"

14. Losing touch

ALREADY ON THE VERY FIRST NIGHT, Anna noticed the loss of touch. It was like losing a sense, like the first veil of mist edging over the cornea, presaging blindness.

She had ceremonially swept the kitchen floor and put a clean cloth on the table; Alan had gone down to the café for fish and chips.

"You want some fish?" he asked Leah on his return, unrolling the newspaper parcel on the kitchen table like a tool-kit.

"I don't eat fish," she replied. "Or any kind of animal."

"Christ," murmured Alan. "Have some chips then."

"I'm not particularly hungry," said Leah, tucking a green scarf more closely around her neck.

Her face was porcelain, nested in the emerald silk. She seemed different, in Alan's presence: reserved, almost prim. Her language and bearing were more adult, and at the same time reminiscent of the Leah from school.

"Let's play cards," suggested Anna, alarmed by the sudden coldness at the table.

She set a bottle of whisky and three glasses on the table. Leah smiled slightly, not taking her eyes off Alan.

"I'm not very good at these things," she said. "What are we playing?"

"Hearts," said Alan, after a pause. "It's really easy."

Anna smiled to herself. Usually, *Black Bitch* was the name of this game. Alan was watching his language.

Leah drank her whisky slowly, with careful sips. As they played, Anna noticed that the air between her own body and Alan's, only centimetres deep, seemed to cool by a few degrees. Tentatively, she placed her fingers over his knuckles on the table. Usually he would turn his hand palm-up and curl his fingers lightly around hers; but now it remained prone on the table like a dead thing. Stubbornly, she left her own hand there, stacked awkwardly on top of his. He did not look at her.

"Joanna, it's you to deal," said Leah.

She withdrew her hand from Alan's and shuffled the cards.

"Not so hard," said Alan. "You'll bend them."

Silence as she dealt. She could still feel the coldness of his hand on her fingertips.

"Clockwise," muttered Alan.

"I know that."

Anna picked up the cards, reshuffled, redealt. Clockwise. Then she sat with her chin on her fist, digging the spikiest ring into her jawbone. She had appalling cards: the queen of spades smiling coldly in profile, the jack of clubs flirting with his thin moustache. They played in turn, the red and black characters telling out their small story. Casually, Leah won the hand.

"Fuck that," said Alan – becoming, it seemed, less shy.

The next round, Leah dealt. Alan was pleased with his cards: Anna saw a little curve of satisfaction at the corner of his mouth, sharp, shaped like a comma or a cut fingernail. She had seen him crease his mouth like that many times, in moments of secret relish: running his fingers along the silky edge of a piece of wood he had just sanded; or buttering a slice of toast in the morning, thinking himself unobserved. It was a feature of his face that, every time, ambushed her with tenderness; and also touched her slyly in the groin: in bed she would always watch – out of one eye, through her lashes, her face too close to his to see much more – for that little new-moon curve.

Now, unthinking, she put out her hand to touch the side of his mouth – in delight, in desire; perhaps also to hide its intimacy from Leah's eyes. But he moved his head at the wrong moment, bending to put a cigarette to his lips: Anna's finger went into his eye. His head snapped back.

"What the *fuck*?"

Frightened, Anna pulled her hand away, as Leah laughed softly from behind her cards.

"Sorry," Anna said.

She held her cards so tightly that her thumbnails bit into their plasticised surfaces. She was shaken; she could not remember hurting him ever before, not by touch. Touching was their most eloquent conversation. When she was sad, she could be comforted by standing behind him and laying her face against the muscles of his back. At night in the dark, she could put her hand directly onto that part of his arm where her fingers fitted best, or that exact warm place at the nape of his neck. Losing this sense of his body, of how to touch it – it would be like losing the power of speech.

She played a card at random. The king of hearts: a warlike and, in this game, a foolish card to play; but nobody was paying much attention. Alan was drawing a long needle of bone from the remains of the fish. As if seeing something happening far away, on the other side of a great valley, Anna watched as he held the bone up before Leah's eyes.

"Isn't that beautiful," he said.

Leah smiled coolly, her wig rustling against the silk of her scarf as she leaned back to observe the bone through narrowed eyes.

"It is," she conceded.

"Some things about an animal you can only appreciate," Alan continued, "when you eat it."

Smiling straight into Leah's eyes, he placed a forkful of the white flesh into his mouth.

Anna gathered the cards and shuffled, snapping their edges loudly with her thumbs.

"Another round?" she asked loudly.

"Oh, I don't think so, I'm pretty tired," said Leah. "Thanks, though. I don't usually like games."

She stood up.

"Wait, Leah, wait," said Anna, who had drunk too much whisky. "I want to ask you something."

Leah waited.

"Do you remember Robbie, from school?"

Leah frowned, smiling at the same time.

"Like I said. I don't remember much from then."

She gave a little wave goodnight, and went to her room. Anna and Alan were left stranded at the kitchen table, the space between them littered with the wreckage of an evening: the empty whisky bottle, scattered cards, a few pallid leftover chips. To her own eyes, Anna's skin looked greenish-pale and greasy.

"Whoops," said Alan, "I'm a bit drunk."

He crumpled the chip paper into a ball and tossed it at the bin. It missed. He got up and fetched it, sat down again, aimed.

"So," he said. "Leah. She doesn't talk much."

"She's shy."

"She's a stuck-up little bitch."

The paper ball landed cleanly in the bin, without touching sides. Alan slapped the table in triumph, and the whisky bottle fell over. Ridiculously, Anna felt tears well in her eyes.

"I was expecting something more ... I don't know," Alan continued. "She's really ... uh, what's the word?"

"I don't know."

"No man, you do know. Not stuck-up, exactly, more ... more like ... you know?" he persisted.

"I don't know," she whispered. "I don't know what you mean."

Leah and Alan were both asleep when Anna left the house the next morning. At work she sat in her small office, hung over, staring at the barely animated octopus. At eleven, she phoned home.

"What's she doing?" she asked immediately.

"Can't say."

"What, she's there in the room with you?"

"Mm-hmm."

"Everything okay? How's your head?"

"Mm. Fine, fine. We're going to go down to the beach."

Anna paused.

"You're taking her to the beach?"

"Is that okay?"

"Well ... no ..."

"Is it a problem?"

"Oh, no, no, that's great." She laughed. "Thanks."

Anna returned the receiver softly to its cradle. She looked down at her hand and saw that she had drawn a dog's face on her foolscap pad, with big teeth. She closed her eyes gently, and found on the inside of their lids a little picture: Alan and Leah, walking side-by-side along a brilliant beach, in a storm of golden sand.

But when she came home that evening, everything was different again: Leah was in the kitchen, chopping garlic with rapid strokes of a large knife. Leeks, carrots, some green things so exotic that Anna could not give them a name. Leah made no mess, scooping garlic peels and carrot-ends with her left hand into the bin as quickly as she produced them with her right. On the kitchen table was a fresh tablecloth, a candle in a saucer and a bottle of expensive red wine; the floor had been swept. Anna felt she was visiting in some stranger's kitchen.

"Hi," said Leah with a smile. "I thought we could do a bit better than fish and chips tonight."

"This is amazing," said Anna, putting her bag down slowly on the floor. "Where's Alan?"

Leah shrugged.

"Gone out," she said. "I think he's had enough of me already."

The two women ate by candlelight. The vegetable bake was delicious, and the wine had no rough edges. Anna felt it sitting like a warm ruby in her stomach, still carrying the candle glow. They spoke about photography, art, work; avoiding the past. But then Leah spoke abruptly:

"Robbie."

Anna looked up.

"Yes?"

"He was the epileptic one."

"Yes." Anna paused. "He drowned. You must remember."

Leah straightened her back and took a deep, measured breath. She held it for a moment; then let it out slowly.

"Of course I remember. I was on the beach with him that night."

"I know."

"How?"

"I saw you – don't you remember?"

Leah shook her head, puzzled. Anna sighed. *Invisible.*

"So what happened?"

Leah hesitated before answering.

"Robbie had a big crush on me. He got this idea to swim – showing off, I suppose. But I didn't want to, I was cold. So I came back to the house and went to sleep." She smiled faintly. "I thought it would be funny – he'd come out of the water and I'd be gone."

"Why didn't you say anything? You just disappeared, afterwards."

Leah shrugged.

"We moved. And I wanted to forget about it. I felt responsible, in a way." She peeled a long piece of wax off the candle. "It was a very sad thing."

Anna gazed at Leah's slim fingers, rolling the wax into a little ball.

Could it be true? A stupid accident, nothing more.

Yes. Of course that's how it was.

The ruby inside Anna's stomach rotated gently in internal candle-light, facets glinting. She looked at Leah and smiled, feeling suddenly hopeful.

"Yes," she said. "Wasn't it?"

Alan woke her when he came home that night. It was very late, and he smelt of the world: alcohol and smoke, and other pungent things she could not name. She snuffed at his skin as he climbed in under the duvet. He did not speak.

"So how was the beach?" she asked eventually; but Alan's eyes were already closed, his breathing even and deep.

Usually, such quiet moments provoked the greatest desire in Anna: she would dip her head and delicately taste the sea salt at Alan's collarbone or below his ribs, the soft skin behind his knees. It was the taste of a marine creature brought up from the deep; not human. Falling asleep with her face against his chest she would imagine herself pulled down by that heavy smell and taste, down to a place of dangerous beauty, dark light, dense air.

But this night, she did not want to touch him. Instead she lay for a long time awake, watching his profile. Eventually he turned his face away from her, like the side of a planet falling away from the sun.

This was how the days went. Anna left the house every morning before the other two got up; from work, she phoned home at intervals, to check on things. Oddly, it was always Alan who answered – it seemed he was spending almost every day at the house.

"Where is she now?"

"She's up on the roof again."

"Doing what?"

"She just sits up there. She watches the sea."

"Did you go down to the beach today?"

"No. It was too windy."

"Is it okay, Alan?" she asked, covering her notepad with intricate ballpoint. Her doodling had become in every sense mechanical: she produced neat diagrams of interlocking cogs, drive-belts, pistons. "You don't mind her being there?"

"I don't mind."

"Why does she never answer the phone?"

"Like I said. She's on the roof, mostly."

"I don't see why you have to run around answering the phone."

There was a long pause.

"So then don't phone every ten minutes," he replied.

Returning in the evenings, she would find Leah cooking. In Anna's absence the flat grew mysteriously cleaner. It started to smell of new things: ginger, floral air freshener, incense, and other sternly feminine scents. On the bathroom shelf stood, mundanely, a contact lens case and a bottle of solution. Anna had imagined Leah storing her lenses like jewels, in a special casket; lined, perhaps, with strawberry-coloured silk.

Another week passed, and Anna started to become irritable. One night she came home to find Leah in a nightgown of red silk, embroidered with many tiny jet beads. She was carefully positioning three tall red candles in a row on the kitchen table. Anna was tired, and annoyed by the theatricality of the scene.

"So how's the job-hunting going?" she asked.

Leah lit all three candles, carefully. She shook the match out before answering.

"I've been very, very busy," she said, putting the dead match back in the box, and the box into a pocket of her robe.

She clasped her hands in front of her and observed the flames, satisfied. The beads glistened like tiny beetles crawling on the fabric of her gown.

"Busy with what?"

"Different things."

"I thought you were so desperate to find work."

Leah leaned forward to shift the central candle fractionally to the right, smiling enigmatically.

"Oh, work … I'll find work. You did."

Yes, but I'm the artist, remember. Avoiding Leah's eyes, she jerked open the fridge door and poured herself a tall glass of iced water. Leah continued:

"I mean, I'd like to do something like your job. Something creative."

There was a pause while Anna watched the sides of the glass mist up.

"I don't know," she said flatly. "It's not so easy, you know."

Her own voice surprised her: so clear and cold.

"Oh, sure – but you could give me some pointers. What equipment to buy. Stuff like that."

Anna took a measured sip of water. It felt as if her insides were rapidly cooling and hardening, like wax.

"Tell me. Why did you come to find me, at the aquarium?"

Leah seemed confused by the question.

"Because we were friends. At school, we were friends," she said, as if this were obvious.

"Oh."

Hard-hearted Anna had another sip, feeling her lips go numb. She found she was enjoying the slight cruelty of the conversation. It was a new feeling, pleasurable even.

"We used to sit together," Leah continued, almost pleading. "You were the only one who talked to me. Don't you remember?"

"I don't remember much from that time."

"But we were friends …"

"I don't remember having friends."

She drank her water slowly, relishing it. But looking up, she saw that an answering chill had crept across Leah's eyes, frosting the gold. And suddenly the water felt too cold in her mouth: like a chemical, like something she should not have drunk.

15. Theft

ANNA DID NOT SING OR PLAY AN INSTRUMENT. When she hummed to herself in the car or the shower, it was simple stuff: bubblegum pop, TV jingles, Christmas carols from long ago. Classical music only made her irritable – all that difficult fervour. She preferred small, clear sounds, easy tunes; silence was the best.

So she felt affronted that afternoon, coming home to loud orchestral music – torrential piano, remonstrating violins – spilling out onto the landing. Anna squinted into a noisy glare: it seemed that all the doors and windows in the flat had been thrown wide open, letting sound and light wash through. She pushed her way into the lounge like a firefighter battling into the heart of a burning building.

Leah was standing in the centre of the room in her underwear. A tiny white vest did not come down far enough to cover her thumbprint navel; the cotton shorts were so thin one could see the shadow of pubic hair, even the cleft of the genitals. She was on one leg, birdlike, the left foot propped against the right knee. Looking up, she took an exaggerated step towards Anna, stepping high over the photographs that scattered the floor, arms spread to balance. Her skin was lightly sheened with sweat, her eyes unfocused, painted impenetrably gold. Leah opened her mouth, and as she did so the music swelled to a brassy clash – a fierce golden sound that she seemed to release like the roar of an angel.

"What?" shouted Anna into the din.

With her big toe, Leah turned down the volume on the stereo at her feet.

"I said hi," she laughed, oddly breathless.

Anna lingered in the doorway. Her clothes were dark, and hung heavily on her shoulders as if she had rocks in her pockets. Glancing at the mirror on the wall next to her, she saw that her eyes were deeply ringed with black. She had not slept well the night before, nor any night for the past week.

Shifting her gaze, she found Leah smiling at her.

"These are mine," Anna said flatly.

"I know, they're fantastic. And look, look what I've done." Leah was excitable, delighted.

"They're my pictures, Leah. You took them from under my bed."

"Oh, you don't mind, do you? Look, isn't this great?"

Leah had pushed the couch back against the wall and laid the prints out on the bare floorboards. Anna was surprised at how many pictures there were, how many square metres: *his back, his arm, his jaw, his foot.* Obscenely intimate things, exposed to such clear sunlight, and to such a brightly golden gaze. Pictures of Alan were interleaved with prints from the aquarium – mostly of the rays and sharks. A mosaic of different varieties of skin: soft and sandpapery, silver and grey, human and other.

"What do you think?" Leah asked. "Kief, hey?"

That stupid schoolgirl slang again.

"I think they're my pictures."

'Well, yes, but look what we can do with them ... I've put them out, see – they fit."

Leah pointed with her bare toe. Her feet were long, delicately boned, as expressive as hands. And indeed, Anna could not deny that the images worked well together: matching textures, echoed shapes; correlations, kinship. Hard to tell, in some places, what was man and what fish.

"They're mine," she repeated, stubbornly.

"So, we can work together. Your images, my designs. We'll collaborate. You can show me what to do."

Anna felt ill.

"I don't know what Alan's going to think about this."

"Oh, he likes it," said Leah. "Don't you?"

She looked up, over Anna's shoulder.

Alan came out from the bedroom. He was wearing a pair of old jeans, no shirt or shoes. He stood at Leah's side, her pointy elbow almost touching his hip. Their proximity to each other made the hairs on Anna's arms rise, under the carapace of her black dress. She stared at him furiously.

"But they're mine, they're of you."

He shrugged:

"So? You're not going to do anything with them. They'll sit under the bed forever."

Vanity, weakness, treachery, she thought; but could say nothing. The music had calmed down now, reduced to a single winding woodwind – oboe perhaps, she wouldn't know. She closed her eyes, and allowed the tune to lead her away down its narrow consoling path.

Now every evening Anna would return from work to find fresh monsters laid out on the lounge floor. Leah had started to make photocopies, multiplying the images with cancerous zeal. Her collages reminded Anna of someone tiling a bathroom floor: that dogged, that obvious. Here and there, some feature – hand or eye – would be tentatively touched up with Indian ink. But Leah did not seem to know how to proceed.

"What do you think, Joanna?" she asked, discontentedly scratching her shoulder-blade with the end of a paintbrush. "What does it need?"

Five identical pictures of dorsal fins were laid out in a row on the floor, evenly spaced like the teeth of a saw. Leah had started colouring them in, very neatly, in pale acid green.

"I think it's nice," said Alan mildly.

"Joanna? What does it need?" Leah repeated, ignoring him.

"How would I know?" Anna replied with dull contempt as she passed through the lounge on her way to the bathroom. "You're the artist."

The next day, Leah returned from the copy shop with another stack of paper: reams of repeating fins and legs and eyes. Soon she ran out of floor, and began to pin pictures up on the walls. To make space, she took the mirrors down, stacking them behind the couch. Anna, watching the bright planes being packed away, numbly did not protest. There had been beautiful things in those mirrors once: they had shown her a body, a face. But that was all going now. Without the mirrors, the room was less bright. The walls turned slowly darker – the photocopies like some kind of dull algae growing inch by inch across the plaster.

"Maybe you should go to an employment agency," suggested Anna at last, arms folded across her chest, rings pressed into her biceps.

Leah, working cross-legged on the floor, looked up with some surprise. She held a cutting knife delicately between thumb and forefinger, as a hairdresser holds a comb. She was busy with photocopies of Alan's eyes, nose, chin. A dreadful hydra stared at Anna with a dozen eyes.

"Oh, but I'm so busy here!" Leah smiled, neatly slicing the nose out of Alan's face. "Do you have any more pictures? I think we need more."

Anna put her hands on her hips and stared at Leah's swift fingers with puzzled obstinacy. All the time, a small voice in the back of her head was saying: *She's doing it wrong. I would do something completely different with that one, you see, like this* ... It was a confident superior voice, one she remembered from art school.

"I don't have any more pictures."

"Well ... can't you take some more?" Leah continued patiently. "I really do think we need some variety here. More angles. More skin."

Anna breathed in deeply, and slowly out, wanting to scream: *More skin?* But she just tightened her folded arms, until the grip she had on herself was quite painful.

"I'll have a look," she murmured, and went to her room.

Alan was there, lying on the bed on his stomach. His arms were tucked awkwardly under his body, so that he looked like a man with missing limbs. Anna sat on the foot of the bed and ran her thumbnail down the sole of his bare foot to make it curl. He rolled over onto his back.

"Hi," he said.

"Have you seen what she's doing?"

He pushed himself up higher against the pillows, frowning.

"Of course."

"So ... what do you think? Aren't they awful?" She was whispering.

"... I don't know."

"What do you mean, you don't know?" her voice rose. "They're hideous! She's cutting up my pictures! Pictures of you!"

"She said she was designing posters, or something. Some work."

"Work? No-one's going to pay her for that crap! I bet you she's never made a poster in her life!"

"They don't look like posters," he said uncertainly. "But I don't know."

"Don't know what?"

"Don't you think they're quite ... creative?"

"Oh, Jesus, creative! They're mine! *Creative!*"

She smacked his toes, hard, with the rings. He pulled his legs up and rolled on his side.

"Well jees. They're your pictures, you tell her about it. I'm sleeping."

"Alan!"

"I'm asleep."

She sighed and went back to the lounge. But Leah was no longer there. Suddenly Anna felt very lonely, with her reflection stripped from the walls – all those lovely silvered pictures of herself. She went into the bathroom and gripped the basin, leaning forward and staring grimly into her own eyes in the mirror. The rings underneath them were very heavy, her face pallid.

Behind her, strange creatures shifted their leathery wings in the rooms of the flat: *bad spells, bad spells.* She closed her eyes and leaned her forehead against the glass, wishing its coolness into her brain. *Smooth silver thoughts, slow smooth silver thoughts, slow as the passage of the ray, silver as the fish angling their flattened bodies in the blue aquarium light ...*

A sound, metal on metal. Anna opened one eye, to see Leah standing in the doorway, bearing in her left hand a paring knife. She smiled and licked something off it with a relish not reflected in her flat golden eyes. Anna sighed, rolled her forehead back against the glass, met her own ordinary gaze. She could not fight against this magic; she could not even raise her voice against it.

"Food's ready," Leah said. "Come and get it."

These days, when Anna called home from work in the middle of the day, the telephone was seldom answered. Perhaps there was a fault in the line: it rang and rang, echoing into an ambiguous silence on the other end – whether the silence of an empty house, of dead people, or of mocking presences who refused to answer, Anna could not tell. Sometimes she thought she could hear strange submarine sounds on the other end: deep-sea groans and hums, distant whale music; radar, telegraph clicks, listeners holding their breath. Or waves, a faraway sound; the ocean rearranging itself. Each time she waited for twenty rings exactly, and then hung up, unsettled.

In the margins of her drawing pad, her doodles were changing character. All by itself, her hand had started drawing hearts again. With daggers through them. And big drops of blood where the daggers went in. She put her head down and banged it softly on her desk, and laughed at her own foolishness.

She found herself unwilling to return to the flat in the evenings, to the complicated thickness of the air there. Always, Alan or Leah seemed to be either sleeping or eating: creatures of torpor and greed and – Leah standing one-legged in the lounge, the scissors shining in her delicate hand – occasional cruelty. She wondered what they did all day, to tire them so. Every evening, it felt as if Alan and Leah had receded further behind volumes of clear water, their forms shifting, eliding, playing tricks on her eyes. Sometimes she imagined, turning the handle, that she was about to swing open not an ordinary front door, but an airlock into a cold submarine world.

She started to delay going home. She walked on the mountain nearly every evening, coming down in failing light. She often took Alan's car, so that she didn't have to catch the train home after dark.

Returning to the flat, Anna would smell of pine needles, damp roots and rocks. Her eyes would be dilated from seeing in the dark, her skin cool. The air in the kitchen where Alan and Leah waited was oily with cigarette smoke and yellow light. They would already be eating, and would watch her enter in silence, food halfway to their mouths.

"You're bleeding," Leah remarked severely one evening.

"Hmm? Oh, I scratched myself."

The blood on her arm was as bright as enamel paint. Her T-shirt was damp with sweat under the armpits and down the back: she had not been so wilfully dirty since childhood.

"Pasta," she noted.

"Alan cooked tonight."

"Ah."

"Good walk?"

"Fine," she said, smiling across the table at a neutral space between these two strangers. "So. Can I have some food?"

Distantly, she heard Leah and Alan speaking, but she did not understand: they talked of city things. Anna was far away, halfway up the mountain, suspended kilometres above their heads.

"Anna?"

"What?"

"I said we were thinking," said Alan.

"Oh."

"I thought we could take Leah to see the whales some time. They're … what's it?"

"Calving," said Leah quickly.

"Ja, calving. At Pringle Bay, or Hermanus maybe."

"We could all go. It'd be fun," said Leah.

Anna ate steadily. They watched her in silence.

"So is that okay? Maybe this weekend, or the next one?" Alan asked.

Anna shrugged.

"Sure," she said, giving herself another big helping of pasta.

It tasted awful, of packet soup and salt.

Some nights Anna was tempted not to come home at all; to curl up in a dark corner of the aquarium and wait for morning, comforted by the night-light of the green tanks. After hours, Anna would linger near the sleepless sharks: their constant movement always soothed her, like white noise. She would lean her hands and then her forehead up against the glass, the fierce creatures patrolling centimetres from her face. It was like standing on the edge of a cliff, looking down at death so easy and near; kept away by nothing stronger than a sheet of glass.

She knew the sharks well by now, as well as she knew Alan's face; and though she had never touched the animals, she knew exactly how their sandpapery sides would feel on her palm. Not as smooth as a lover's skin perhaps, but potently alive.

In sleep she was visited by strange new dreams: fish-men hanging in rustling gardens of kelp; Alan, transformed into a long, white, cartilaginous creature moving swiftly through the water, his eyes wide open and fixed ahead of him. That dream frightened her. And she did not like the one in which she waited on a beach, while Alan dragged from the sea the skeleton of a whale. In the dream she started to cry, and Alan came to where she sat on the sand. But instead of comforting her, he pulled from his mouth a long white splinter of bone, and offered it to her with a smile.

Waking, she would lie watching Alan through half-closed eyes. Wondering how he would look, perhaps, with a school of little fish passing through his face. Wrapped in bandages of grey-green weed. Sunk, perhaps, in deep water, tiny bubbles in the lashes of his eyes.

16. Uncoupling

AFTER WORK THAT THURSDAY, gripped by a fierce energy, Anna ran up the mountain from the gate at Constantia Nek, so fast her legs were shaking when she reached the top. She ducked under the fence around the high reservoir and sat for an hour or more next to the water, hugging her knees and watching the reflections, seeing creatures curling and crawling beneath the mirror surface.

A man made his way slowly down from the far stone houses, across the dam wall, and towards her along the rim of the water. His overalls were luminous orange. He seemed in no hurry, pausing to toss a pebble far and high like a warning shot. Together, they watched it splash near the centre of the dam, and waited for the first ripple to touch the shore. Then he approached.

"You can't come in here," he said.

"I know."

"Didn't you see the sign on the fence?"

"I did."

His uniform was brand new, so bright its colour hurt her eyes; perhaps he was wearing it for the first time. A pale blue tattoo peeked from under one hot orange sleeve, indistinct on the back of his hand.

"It's not allowed."

"I know."

"Sorry."

She smiled at him, grateful for the correctness and courtesy of their exchange: so straightforward, so easy. She stood, and sighed, and allowed him to escort her to a different hole in the fence, which he politely pulled wider for her to climb through.

"Thank you," she said.

He waved; she waved back, and started back down the way she had come. It was getting colder. Darkness fell as she was halfway down the zigzag forester's road. The track was densely fenced in with pine trees; she could sense the warm bodies of birds asleep in the branches above her head. Scorning the miniature flashlight she kept on her key-ring, she walked by the pale shine of the concrete underfoot. Her eyes felt huge in her face, hungry for scraps of light.

She nearly fell over the figure in the dark, and cried out. Her voice was immediately dampened by the wall of trees. The woman sat by the side of the path, her feet tucked together and her hands in her lap, as if waiting. Her face was in darkness. A piece of clothing showed from beneath her top, a soft white triangle under her chin. She did not move or speak.

"Hello," said Anna, her heart fast.

The woman said nothing. Anna felt in her pocket for the key-ring. The torch's beam reduced the forest to a narrow well of light.

"Is everything okay? Are you hurt?"

The woman raised her head, showing a small thin face of indeterminate age and colour, a polished bronze in the torchlight. She was not dressed for walking: she wore soft city shoes, a pale dress, a knitted cardigan. Her hair was hidden in something dark, a hat or scarf. In the torchlight her eyes glistening yellowly like an animal's. Anna dipped the beam away from them apologetically.

"Where are you going?" she asked.

The woman pointed silently up the path. It was another forty minutes' steep walk up the path to the top, where the reservoirs were, and houses, and people living.

"Do you stay up there?"

The woman turned her head towards the darkness, as if she had seen a movement or heard her name called. Then she rose calmly to her feet, brushed off her skirt, and without another glance started up the hill. Her footsteps were silent on the pine needles. Anna watched until the slight figure disappeared entirely into the darkness.

Anna switched off the torch; but the night had become frighteningly black. Turning it on again, she felt revealed – the pool of yellow light around her was intimate and slightly shameful, like something emitted by her own body. *Danger is here, is near,* she thought, straining to see beyond the limits of her own lit circle. She was no longer a forest animal, seamlessly part of the dark: something was looking in, into her room of torchlight that had no walls. She started down.

She must live up there, in one of those stone houses at the top next to the reservoirs. A forestry worker's wife, perhaps. Maybe she has missed a lift up; any minute now I will see the headlights of a truck beaming zigzag up through the trees, the engine shockingly loud, and I will stop them as they come round the bend and tell them to pick her up on the way. And they will laugh and say oh ja we know her, she is waiting for us.

She could see the city now between the trees – points and rows of lights – but cloud was coming over the mountain, and it would rain soon. *Should I have followed her? Or offered her my jersey? Surely she could not get lost, not on this wide road. What if she is mad, wandering up here alone – a crazy woman? But why should she be crazier than I, here in this place at the same late hour?* As she came out of the trees, Anna switched off the torch again so as to approach the city in darkness. Then she was at her car, getting into it, pulling away.

The rain started up heavily as she drove the long way to Muizenberg in the dark. She was startled by the lights of oncoming traffic on the highway, wheels spinning up water. The landscape slipped past at ferocious speed, the wet bridges and roadworks racing towards some carnage, some savage rendezvous on the road behind her. Anna drove carefully, trying to slow everything down. Her thighs and buttocks were clenched tight on the seat, her hands gripping the wheel as if soldered there – a metal person, compelled into human action.

The highway left the suburbs and lifted over the unlit, tree-filled space of Wynberg Park. Suddenly from the darkness a man ran out in front of the car. His body was bent into the rain and his clothes were the same sodden grey as the road. Swerving to miss him, she glimpsed for the briefest moment his smeared face turned towards her – grey skin, dull unfrightened eyes. With what seemed deliberate anger he slammed a palm onto the roof of the car with a thud as he spun out of her path.

She corrected her skid and drove on, her feet shaking uncontrollably on the pedals. The man had disappeared in her rear-view mirror, slipping between the grey veils of rain. The world was breaking apart, grey ghosts entering through the cracks.

Alan was sitting at the kitchen table, cutting notches into its edge with a silver penknife. She stood in the archway, breathing heavily from her run up the stairs. He looked up at her, the knife a narrow leaf-shape of brightness in his hand.

"You're late."

The words escaped him violently, as if he had been holding his breath for hours. His face was finely creased, the skin a layer of glass that had been crazed in spiderweb lines. Anna was still trembling from the near-accident, and the room itself was tremulous, tables and chairs and photographs threatening to fly apart at a loud word. Feeling seasick, she sat down.

Alan was smoking: smoke seeped from him, leaking through the faults in his skin. He stubbed out the cigarette in the glass ashtray in front of him, watching his hand as if it belonged to another person.

"Where've you been?" Crushing and crushing the end of his cigarette.

"Up on top."

Deliberately, he stood and went to the window. His body seemed dense with shadow. Anna thought of black pigment dissolving into a glass of water: darkness diffusing from him.

He used to seem so bright.

She went to him, and laid her hands flat on his back, feeling the electric hum coming through her palms: like laying her hands on a running engine, on the metal casing of a hot machine of many moving cogs. The room grew quickly dimmer around them, shadow furniture piling up around the real. Alan's darkness clung to her, smelling of smoke, paint, oil; of turpentine and fire.

"What's wrong?" she said.

There was a long silence.

"Nothing," he said at last softly. "Nothing."

"Where is she?"

"Asleep already. We're leaving in the morning – early."

Her heart lurched.

"Leaving."

"For the weekend. Remember – Pringle Bay, the whales? You were going to take the day off work tomorrow."

Yes, she remembered. *Moonlit waves, a silver beach; whales out there somewhere, invisible in the dark water.*

"I don't think I'll come."

"Why not?"

She was silent.

"Why not?" he repeated.

"There's too much to do at work. I must put up this new penguin display over the weekend."

Alan's muscled shoulders were rigidly still. Anna bent and touched the back of his neck with her lips. She felt the tension of his mouth as she passed her fingers lightly and blindly over it; but she could not read his expression.

"I'm tired now," she whispered, suddenly too exhausted to think. She would face the further fracturing of the world tomorrow, in daylight.

"I'm tired too."

It was nine o'clock, ludicrously early; but holding hands like a frail elderly couple they went into the bedroom and stretched out on the bed, gripping each other softly elbow to wrist. The angle of her arm was uncomfortable, but he would not let her go. After a while, when she was sure he was asleep, she withdrew her arm gently and tucked it at her side. *Uncoupling.*

She felt alert and cool. When the back of her foot touched Alan's leg, she pulled away, startled: his skin was so hot, burning up. She sat up and switched on the lamp. His face was set into the severe absorption of the dreamer: eyes moving quickly under their soft lids. Not for the first time, Anna felt an impulse to peel back his lids and watch for herself his dull secret slideshow. Or did Alan have other dreams, lurid, kaleidoscopic; dreams he had never told her?

She turned off the light and lay back on her side of the mattress. But it seemed she was metamorphosing into something sleepless, cold-blooded, reptilian. Her skin made a dry rustling sound against the sheets when she moved.

At three she rose from the bed. In the passageway, she saw a bar of light under Leah's door: thin and precious, like the light reflected off hidden treasure. So Leah was also awake, listening to the night sounds. While Alan visited his grey dream country, the females of the species were wide-eyed, tracking with their heightened hearing his every mutter and snore. He seemed suddenly soft and human to Anna; vulnerable to such wakeful creatures as themselves.

She shivered, and passed through into the darkened lounge, careful to make no sound. In the moonlight, the photos laid out on the floor were glossy squares, like the shed scales of a huge glass-skinned fish. She could feel the eye of the sea looking in at the kitchen window. Although the sky was dark, the sea seemed to retain a thin greenish luminosity – the light of the deep world shining faintly through to the surface. Strange phosphorescent creatures swam down there – great fish, sea serpents, mysteries. Out to sea, she could see the sparks of a few solitary fishing boats, and one fragile moving raft of lights that signified a big trawler or battleship passing. Anna marvelled at them: people, alive, out there on the back of the deep.

The flat was quiet except for the tick and hum of the fridge in the kitchen, and the rough-edged beat of the clock above the couch: a brush slapping softly on a drumhead. And behind that, a bigger broader rhythm: the waves pulling in and out from the shore. Anna felt for the pulse in her wrist: it seemed frail and inconstant compared to the ocean, to time.

She was suddenly afraid. Quietly, standing in her T-shirt in the middle of the dark lounge, she began to cry. And stopped again almost immediately: she never cried loudly, or for long. She wiped her nose and eyes on her T-shirt, and pressed her cold rings against her mouth.

Moving soundlessly back towards the bedroom, Anna saw that the light was out in Leah's room. There was something on the floor preventing the door from shutting – a dark spineless thing, a shed snake skin. It was Leah's bikini top. Standing an arm's length away, Anna stretched out a hand, and with the very tips of her fingers pushed the door open: it submitted, falling away from her with a soft complaint.

Leah had pushed her sheets off, and lay on her left side. Her body was lean and smooth and grey in the half-light. Anna could count the knobs of her spine, each cupped with a soft brushstroke of shadow. She could not see Leah's face: she had tucked it down into the armpit of one outflung arm, finding shelter in her own body – as cats do in sleep, and birds, and other graceful animals.

Anna moved her spread fingers back towards her face; and the door closed over that sleeping scene, following the movement of her hand. At that moment, a heavy rain started up, the loud drops on the roof a relief after the tense ticking silence. She could move freely now, without fear of being heard.

She got back into bed next to Alan, and lay dreaming and waking and sliding back into dream, surrounded by the rain. It was a constant rushing static, like a swarm of small moist-winged creatures trying to get in.

Alan's skin was a soft grey in the underwater light from the street lamp, phantom raindrops creeping over the contours of his body. He did not appear to be breathing. Anna wanted to reach out a hand to check, but was afraid to wake him. Instead she lay very still, watching, until she could detect the fractional rise and fall of his chest.

At six the sky grew lighter and the rain paused. Anna rose and dressed, and left for work without touching him again.

17. The worm turns

THAT DAY, ANNA BECAME ILL AT WORK. Her head ached, and there was an odd, full feeling in her chest, like indigestion or anxiety. Shortly before twelve, she left for home. *The worm turns*, she thought, walking to the station, pressing her abdomen with her fingertips. She had never quite understood that expression, but that was what it felt like: something cold and slippery and alive inside her.

Both cars were still parked outside the flat. Peering into Alan's, she saw a leaf-green cardigan, small enough to fit a child, on the passenger seat. The sleeves were rounded and naturally arranged, as if arms had just been withdrawn from their warm tubes.

Puzzlingly, the flat was empty. In the hallway was a neat pile, ready to go: Alan's rucksack, Leah's satchel, cooler-bag, surfboard. The bedroom was in a mess, with a full ashtray on the floor and the duvet spilling off the bed. Anna stared at its folds, queasily trying to decipher from its twists the history of the last few hours. It looked like the innards of a large bloodless animal that had died in the night.

She felt like a trespasser – these daytime rooms belonged to other people. On the way through to the kitchen, she walked deliberately over the pictures on the floor, disturbing their arrangement. Her head felt bad, so bad.

A hand of patience was laid out on the kitchen table. The faces of the kings and queens were heraldically stern in the cold light, their eyes on her as she crossed the room to the kitchen cupboard, looking for the Panados. As she bent to wash the pills down with tap water, she saw that someone had left the back door unlocked. She straightened and stood for a moment, wiping her mouth with the back of her wrist and considering, before opening the door and stepping out onto the fire-escape.

There was no one above or below her in the silver cage, no bag positioned on the stairs like a signpost. She ascended towards a cold white sky. The roof was puddled from the night's rain. Uneasily, she knew she was missing something, some clue hidden in the familiar shapes and angles. Then she saw it: the padlock on the door of her old darkroom was open, hung neatly on the hasp.

A door in a dream, always approached and never entered.

She went silently towards it and laid an eye to the painted wood, peering through one of the gaps between the boards that had once been covered in black fabric. The red light-bulb was off; the interior was an indistinct theatre of movement, dim shapes without substance or colour. The cracks in the door let the light through in narrow slivers. She saw a section of concrete floor, darkened with a slick of something wet, like oil or blood. Then a sudden body: a thin line of light laid over a man's shoulder, altering as he turned, curving over a heavy cheek, nose, chin. It was a metal face, immobile, eyes slitted. The brass Buddha opened its mouth slightly and licked its lips.

Movement again, reversals of position, flesh of a finer texture. A girl's back, striped with light: sharp shoulder blades, narrow buttocks like a boy's, naked. She might be twelve years old. Her white vest had been pulled over her head and hooked over her thin forearms, as if binding the wrists. Big hands emerged out of the darkness to grasp her waist – long middle fingers nearly touching across the small of her back. The fingernails were very black against the girl's skin.

She turned, and a stripe of light illuminated one golden eye. It seemed to look straight through the crack in the door to meet Anna's gaze. Then, with the sound of a great gong being struck – some resoundingly heavy metal object falling over and rolling – the entwined bodies blundered backwards and sideways into the dark and out of sight.

Anna pulled away from the peepshow darkness, stepped back and stared straight up at the cold sun as if to burn the images off her corneas. But still there was darkness in her stomach, behind her eyes.

She turned and fled down the fire-escape, down past the open kitchen door, feet loud on the metal treads – *eleven, eleven, eleven* – all the way down.

Running down a random side-street, she came to a park, with slides and swings. She swung her legs over the low fence, crossed the grass and climbed the jungle gym, right up to the top. From the other side of the park, a skinny black dog watched her out of one eye, scratching its jaw with a hind leg.

Leah, Alan.

Alan?

She had not recognised him. Of course those had been his hands, his face: she knew them by heart. But he was changed, a stranger now – living in a foreign place where she had never been, speaking a new language. She pressed her face against a cold crossbar, shutting out the light with her arms.

It was a while before she could look around. Although the sun was out, no children played on the damp slides or sat in the puddles collected in the car-tyre swings. Everything was painted red, yellow, blue – always the bright primaries, as if these were the only colours in a child's world. The black dog had edged closer.

The jungle gym was made of metal poles. Her feet were braced against a blue crossbar. Her left hand gripped a yellow rung, her right a red. *Strange, that my grown-up body fits here so well.* The paint was tough stuff, thick municipal enamel: her teeth had left no marks in it.

A park was not a bad place to be – she felt safe among these elemental shapes and colours. It was maths: cubes, circles, arcs. The red and the yellow bars at right angles to the blue. The merry-go-round rotating endlessly around its fixed point. *It's all proof of something, some theorem I can't quite put my mind to; but it's simple, quite straightforward, if I could just remember* ... The soft dazed voice of a teacher whose face she could no longer recall was speaking in her head: *proof of parallel lines, quadrilateral.* For the first time she recognised the chanting, spell-like quality of the words, the calm of those precise constructions.

"Pythagoras, hypotenuse," she said to the dog.

She would wait here; until nightfall, if necessary, or even through until the next day. It might rain again, but that would be okay: she liked the rain's soft static. Perhaps it would fill the gaps that had opened up inside her head.

18. Darkhouse

FROM A DISTANCE, she could see that Leah's car was gone from the parking lot, and that the lights were off in number six. The lighthouse was inverted now, a darkhouse, projecting beams of shadow. Anna imagined strange animals congregating up there, knocking down the furniture, peering from the high windows. She clenched her ringed fists in her pockets and swore when she realised: her keys were locked inside.

Round the back of the building, then, and up the fire escape: *eleven steps, turn, eleven* ... but the kitchen door was also, of course, locked. Irresolute on the metal mesh landing, Anna felt a cold prickle on the back of her neck as the rain started up again. Long hard shudders ran from her scalp down her forearms, lifting goosebumps. She took the last flight of stairs up to the rooftop at a run. Out to sea, veils of rain proceeded across the surface of a grey ocean. Averting her eyes from the darkroom door, she went to stand very carefully on the edge of the roof. Below her, about a metre down and half along, the bathroom window had been left ajar.

Just like getting into a cold swimming pool, she told herself: *don't think at all for the moment of the jump. Then after that you cannot stop, even if you want to.*

She breathed deeply, turned around and, gripping the edge of the roof, lowered herself onto that impossibly narrow ledge, slippery with rain. Not looking, she felt for the drainpipe, stepped down again, and found the windowsill with one foot. After prising the window further open with her toe, she had space to get the other foot onto the ledge ... and was safe, sitting on the sill with air at her back and thighs trembling. She slid in quickly. As she dropped to the floor of the bathroom she banged her elbow hard on the edge of the basin.

Clenching her teeth against the pain, Anna stared into the full-length bathroom mirror with the ornate gilt frame. It was the elongating mirror, the one that made her look leggy and lean, as if stretched like Alice by her drop from the roof. She waited for a long moment, listening, clutching her elbow, holding her own agonised gaze. The silence was barely creased by the distant surf.

Something turned inside her with a heavy click, like the mechanism of an old-fashioned light switch: a single decisive motion, a latch falling into place. Her headache had gone.

She needed to rest; but the bedclothes smelled of sweat and smoke. That rank scent was also in her clothes, her hair, on her skin: Alan's smell, not her own. She took off her clothes and went naked through to the bathroom to wash the odour off.

In the shower, she let the water run cold mercury fingers down her back and between her breasts. She washed her body vigorously all over – in the crotch, particularly, she wanted to be clean and cold – and rubbed it dry with one of the purple towels. They were folded in the cupboard under the basin, where she had hidden them from Leah.

Also under the basin was a box of old unused things: facecloths and dusty plastic bottles of talc. Catching a glint of green glass, Anna dug down into the box and found a heavy perfume bottle – an unopened gift from an aged aunt. She pulled out the stopper and sniffed at the greenish oily stuff. It was called *Sea Spray*, and smelled pungent and salty-sweet, like kelp. She poured some out onto her palms, and touched her fingers to her wrists and her temples. Then she anointed her ankles, stomach, thighs, shoulders. The alcohol in the scent evaporated off her skin like the vapour off dry ice.

Cool temples. Cool hands. Cool breasts, nipples like pebbles. She liked this chilled hard body: a fish, a frozen woman, a statue sunk beneath the surface of a lake. She would refuse to be warmed.

Over this marble skin she put clean clothes: jeans and an old baggy T-shirt, faded red with a Chinese tiger in black on the front. Its striped tail curled over her right shoulder and down onto her back. The perfume was strong under the clothes: now she did not smell like Alan, or herself, or any human thing. Rather like some new being, young and raw.

She opened the windows to feel the cool salt air blowing in from the sea. There were things to do.

She turned her attention to the pictures littering the floor and walls. They did not please her.

"Horrible," she said, aloud. And then again: "Horrible," smiling at the sound of her own voice.

Anna had always been a quiet speaker. Sometimes she imagined her words as the scratchings of a hard pencil, a 3HH perhaps, the sketches she made so light they were barely discernible. But this new voice was of a different material. It had a dark melting quality, like pastel, leaving a rich mark that was impossible to ignore. She experimented, trying out different silly things: accents, monologues, jokes. All those things she always should have said.

She stripped the walls and stacked Leah's ugly pictures in a corner. Then she examined her weapons, laying them out along one wall: ink, crayons, scissors, glue, tape, ballpoint pens, pencils.

"Not enough."

Crawling on her stomach under the bed, she unearthed her materials from the old days at art school. The box was heavy, and she had to kick and pull it across the floorboards into the lounge.

On top was a flat tin containing charcoal sticks, choked with black dust. She placed it to one side. Underneath lay a large cream-coloured envelope. A cool finger of memory brushed, lightly, against the back of Anna's skull. The envelope was thick, slightly textured, unmarked. Her fingertips tingled, as if she could feel secrets wriggling like little worms under the skin of the paper. The flap had glued itself down with time, and she had to tear it open again.

She put her hand in and pulled out a small round mirror. The face she caught briefly in its tarnished surface was one she barely recognised: an unkempt woman with fierce shadows under her eyes. She laid the mirror to one side, with grim care, as if the glass had sharp edges.

There was something else in the envelope. A rectangular piece of white cardboard. She pulled it out and turned it over, counting under her breath: *one two three.*

A picture.

It was not the solemn icon she remembered. This thing was a child's crude mess: black and blue scribblings. A paper scrap had been cut from a magazine and gummed to the card. Most of the glue had come off, and the picture was flapped back to show the words of the article printed on the reverse. Carefully she smoothed it down with her thumb. *Four five six.*

A little boy in his cricket togs.

The rest of the picture was a fiercely dense surface of ink and lead: deeply scored, the paper rubbed to a shine by the pressure of the marks. Here and there a gouge where the pencil lead had broken. Without warning, Anna remembered pressing the point of a pair of geometry compasses into her own forearm. She had forgotten how she used to do that; how she had once possessed such violence.

She placed the picture on the floor and laid her hand briefly over it – *a grown-up hand: look at these clean, unbitten fingernails* – and waited a moment, until the trembling ceased. Sitting

117

back on her haunches, she rubbed her charcoal-smudged fingers on her jeans and sighed, staring at the face of the boy.

A powerful thing, this little picture. A bad spell.

She thought:

I can do better now.

"Red," she said, touching the paintbrush to a photograph of Alan's face like a wand of blood.

Pictures were coming to her quickly, and she executed them with fierce focus. She was precise, controlled: with a steel ruler she measured between two points and scored a shallow incision with a craft knife. The line connected a point on Alan's breast, through his nipple, to the dead centre of the eye of a fish in a different picture. A tuna fish: pelagic, of the deep sea.

"Pythagoras," she muttered in the fading light.

She rubbed black charcoal dust into the cut, like ash into a wound. If you did that to real skin, it would heal, the skin growing back in raised scars. In some cultures this would be considered beautiful.

Here was Alan's face, forearm laid across his eyes. Lips sunburnt and cracked, drawn back from those white even teeth. Suddenly remembering him licking his lips in the tiger light of the darkroom, she filled that mouth with black paint. It dripped down onto his chin like blood. A childish thing, like drawing a moustache on a politician's face in the newspaper. Anna smiled.

Another: a large black-and-white print of Alan's back. His arms and head were tucked away out of sight, tightening the beautiful smooth expanse of skin across the spine. Around his neck, the links of a thick silver chain. Creeping over the left shoulder were four fingers of the right hand, with their four dirty fingernails. The tip of the thumb was a pale nub that looked somehow obscene, caught in the crook of his neck.

Her hands on him, there, at the small of his back.

She tore his spine right out of the photo. Clean murder, blood-

118

less torture and dismemberment. And then a slower reconstitution, a recombination, a painstaking healing.

The pictures were out on the floor again, but it was a different jigsaw puzzle now: a map of a foreign landscape, full of ambiguous structures, highways, earthworks, foundations. She was building a world, cutting and pasting and touching it up, inch by slow inch, like a particularly conscientious god.

Outside, the wind was strong, and the surf sounded loud and near, as if it broke on the walls of the building. But she was safe: she had locked all the doors, closed the windows and bolted them. Nothing could enter, storm or animal or any other visitor. The phone rang every now and then, but she left it. The shrill sound, rather than irritating, added urgency to her work – like far-off sirens, or burglar alarms in distant houses.

As evening came, she left the main lights off, but lit candles and placed them at intervals across the floor, letting the white wax melt onto the paper. Although the windows were closed tight shut, the flames still discovered a secret breeze, making the pictures shiver. As she added layers of texture, the shadow patterns became more uneven and interesting, with lit ridges, dark cracks and pools. The glue and paint dried slowly, making the paper buckle like the surface of a small sea.

Just before dawn she curled up on the couch and slept. She dreamt a long heavy body on top of her, like a dog or big cat. She pushed her face and her hands deep into its hot fur, searching for the hollow, the weak patch, the site of damage; but there was none.

Waking abruptly in the late morning, she was immediately alert, with impatient hands.

She worked intently through the day, pausing only for cups of coffee and handfuls of dry muesli. In the daylight, the overall plan of the pictures seemed more organic: less a landscape or map, more a diagram of an animal's body. She felt like a palaeontologist, assembling ancient bones.

119

But now the body was becoming almost human – one long contour, that had seemed the night before to be a coastline, with bays and inlets, now more resembled the gentle slope of hip and waist. And there, inland, those soft parallel strokes or bars, they could be ribs emerging … it was a giant, stretched out on the floor of the lounge as if asleep. His head faced the kitchen and the sea, while the toes of his right foot extended out towards the entrance hall. The tiny picture of Robbie sat in the region of the heart. The rest of the body was still unclear, requiring work.

Other objects were incorporated: pieces of one of Alan's cigarette boxes; a length of his silver wire; spare blades for his knife. Shiny things, curios and lucky packet trinkets. When she stamped his sunglasses beneath her heel they made a satisfying sound, crunching like the body of a big insect. She shattered the little mirror as well, and knitted the broken pieces into the fabric of the picture – as if she was stitching together a fancy garment, a special suit for the giant.

That night, working by the small light of the candles, Anna began to sense that she was not alone in the flat. *There, listen*: a shallow breathing, very soft. Something asleep, a big torpid creature; a lion lying dreaming on the double bed. A shark hanging in the bath-tub, white, silent, moving its tail slightly side to side to stay afloat. Cats licking their paws in the kitchen. A snake coiled around the faucets in the shower, cold on cold. Creatures breathing, and others holding their breath. *Listen.*

Anna did not feel afraid. She was one of the animals now, prowling long-legged across this landscape of skin; clawing with her nails, hissing, snarling. Looking down at the front of the T-shirt she had worn for days (*two, three?*), she saw the Chinese tiger reaching out a clawed paw to rake her breast. She felt hard, as if there were muscles swelling under her skin, contracting of their own accord; as if she could take someone's face in one hand and crush it. She felt *wild*.

She woke up hungry. In the fridge she found a days-old potato salad which she ate, methodically, cleaning the last fragments from the bowl with her fingers. There was nothing to drink except water and beer: two six-packs of Windhoek. She took a can and downed it quickly, although it was still morning.

All through the day, she was plagued by the ringing telephone. Angrily she refused it; but it would start up again ten minutes later, in fevered counterpoint to her work. At last, late at night, it stopped. By then she was on the last beer. She sipped it slowly as she paced the perimeter of the lounge, examining her creation. It seemed that her work was done.

It looked like many things, depending on the angle of the gaze. From a standing position, it was a picture of a man, a giant. But if she lay down and put her cheek to the floorboards, she became the giant and it a landscape, with miniature rivers and valleys, and mountain ranges eclipsing others from the view.

But it was also like the floor plan of an ancient city, a city built in the shape of a man. All the houses in her city had their roofs removed, and in each room and chamber and courtyard was a different thing: an object, a little dream, a tableau as bright as the windows of the advent calendars she remembered from her childhood.

Here, in one window: Alan, his shoulder-blades fused to the fleshy wings of a ray like a submarine angel, two creatures sharing a spine. Here: Alan's body transformed into the gnarled hook of a seahorse from the waist down. Alan very small, lost in a jungle of sepia kelp. And here: his face, wrapped in weed; Alan, drowning, tortured, wracked by strange metamorphoses.

She went down on her haunches to be closer; she crouched, she crawled over the surface of her creation, touching it with her fingers. *I made them*, she thought with wonder; *these animals*. The pictures seemed to move slightly, a soft malevolent rippling, twisted by unseen tides. A long snaking tail like a wisp of afterbirth; scales glistening. The images shifted minutely in the corners of her eyes, like a shoal of fish moving synchronously: a hundred sleek shapes flashing silver, all at once.

She stretched out on her stomach, belly to belly with the giant, the paint still wet. Right in front of her face was the very first picture, the one of Robbie; embedded now, nested in pigment, paper, glue, time. She lowered her life-size face to his, the size of a fingerprint; softly she touched his forehead with the tip of her nose.

Sleep came easily that night: she lay waiting for it only a short time, stretched out on the map, the paper man, the city. As the last candle drowned in its own wax, she felt her brain spinning backwards in her skull: like a fishing-reel after the line has broken and the fish swum free ... backwards and backwards until it spun right off the edge of some hazy internal cliff and down onto a grey beach ...

And she was kneeling beside his body. Alan was naked, his skin the colour of the sand that had silted around him. Everything was the same grey in the silence: the sand, the flat sea, the sky. His hair was swept straight up like a black fan, as if he was falling through water. There was a residue of sand in his open mouth and his eyes were rolled back in his head. She tried to reach out and close his lids, as she had seen done in movies; but it was as if her hand had no substance – it was ghostly and translucent, and when she tried to move his eyelids her fingers could not find purchase on his skin. She knew with a cold dread that they were in his grey country now, with the medicine bottles, the razorblades: the dead gallery of Alan's dreams.

Looking up, she saw that Leah knelt on his other side. Her hair was wet and long, and she smiled at Anna with contained mischief, softly placing one finger on her lips. Shhh.

19. Sink or swim

ANNA OPENED HER EYES in a room full of space and light. For a while she lay contemplating the flesh of her own outstretched hand: the blue-veined wrist looked tender and delicate, as if it belonged to some other, younger girl. Her forearm was striped with regular golden lines – it was a moment before she realised it was sunlight, filtered through the venetian blinds.

She remembered lying in her mother's bed as a child, sun coming through the stained glass window in unfocused squares of red and blue. She used to imagine that the light had stained her skin – so that she might get up and walk away, still glowing with fuzzy coloured shapes.

She was half-asleep again, wondering if they could do tattoos like that – just patches of soft-edged beautiful colour – when the telephone erupted. Anna scrambled to her hands and knees, heart racing as if a gun had gone off next to her face. When the ringing died at last, she found she was kneeling on an expanse of paper, naked. She could not recall taking off her clothes. Her body was smudged with paint and dusted with black charcoal, and she smelt strange. She stood shakily, and went to stand over the phone in the corner, waiting. The ringing began again: a terrible sound, which she silenced by lifting the thing to her ear.

"Anna?"

The man's voice was harsh and impatient. She held the receiver a little away from her face and frowned.

"Who is this?"

"Me."

"Who?"

"*Me*. Christ. Where've you been all weekend?"

Anna held the receiver even further away, then put it down on the coffee table. Eventually the faint, angry spitting sounds were replaced by a steady buzz. She stared at what lay on the floor.

A shadow man was at her feet, one arm outstretched, bruised-blue fingers almost touching her bare toes – as if, in despair, he had abandoned an attempt to crawl away through the kitchen. Now he was quiet, all the strength bled out of him. Suddenly, she remembered Alan's grey body on the beach; the dread and guilt of the strange dream flooded her like heavy water.

Did I do this? Did I make this pitiful thing?

Gently, she lifted one of the drooping paper arms a few centimetres off the floor. It was cool, and surprisingly heavy with its layers of tape and paint and glue. Somehow the weight made it seem more real: the actual skin of a tattooed giant. In places the paint had cracked, and some of the photographs were coming adrift.

Kneeling, she laid her hand ceremonially on the figure's chest, trying to summon some appropriate memory, some final words.

How did he look? What was his smell? His voice, what was that like?

She remembered the smooth skin on his back and his chest, its warm flex and shift. She remembered the intimate sounds that came from his stomach at night. His breathing. She remembered how, when she ran her hand along his arm, the hairs would rise on her own.

But that was all. She tried in vain to recall something Alan had said, some thought that was uniquely his; but she could not put her mind to it. The only things that came to her were his colourless dreams: *a grey beach; a packet of razor-blades*. It was as if he had left his body years ago, without her noticing. As if she had held a shed skin, thinking she had the snake. As if all she had known of him was what she could touch.

Anna did not want to look at this paper corpse. Like a guilty lover, she quickly pulled on her clothes and slipped out through the back door, needing to breathe clean air.

Up on the roof, she went to stand right at the edge, her bare toes curling over the drop. She stretched her arms to the sky and breathed in deeply.

Her body stank: stale sweat and beer and cheap perfume. And under that, the fragrances of paint and glue and pastel crayons. Those art-room smells – they used to make her mouth water. *Long ago now, long ago, when I was young.*

It was early, and there was great stillness. No swell, no breeze, no cars on the road.

Cessation. Silence. An end to motion.

And she very nearly let it go then: toppled, slipped, released herself to gravity. As easy as falling asleep; as a stone dropped in water. But a small voice interrupted:

Not now, it said. *They're coming.*

The Mazda was indeed turning into the parking lot, pulling up directly below her. Instinctively she stepped away from the edge, ran down the fire-escape and back into the kitchen, closing the door behind her – as if that would keep them out.

There was very little that she needed. She considered her box of photographs, her purple towels, the clothes of ancient black and newer blue. But no, no: she could leave all that behind. The camera? *Yes, even the camera.*

Already she could hear them clattering up the front stairs, loud as soldiers. She grabbed her wallet, a pair of old tackies. At the back door she knelt to put the shoes on; and all at once they were through the front door, into the echoing passageway. Anna soundlessly knotted the laces. Now they were in the lounge, they could

125

see the pictures, the empty beer bottles, the mess of candlewax ... agitated voices, his deep, hers high; incoherent.

Alan stepped into the kitchen archway, and she froze – *a tree, a stone*.

But she was safely hidden behind the kitchen table. Or perhaps he looked straight at her, and simply could not see.

"She's gone to work already," he said, turning away. "Can you believe it."

He leaned his hip lazily against the archway, shoving a hand into the back pocket of his jeans. Looking at the nape of his neck – exposed now as he bent to fit a cigarette to his lips – she could remember the feel of the vertebrae and the fine hair under her palm. But all that was over now. If she touched him, she knew his body would feel inert: a styrofoam shape covered in dead skin.

Leah stepped neatly out from behind Alan's greater bulk, in one movement placing her hand on the small of his back, under the T-shirt. He arched his spine slightly at her touch. *So*, Anna observed: *her hand fits there too*. They had not seen her yet.

Suddenly bold, she stood noiselessly and curled a finger around the door-handle, like the trigger of a gun behind her back. The handle turned with the faintest of creaks. Leah looked up.

There was moment of stillness, in which Anna noticed small things: there was sand on Leah's bare feet, as if she had just walked in off the beach. A strand of the long hair at her temple was caught in the corner of her mouth, like a thin crack across her face; Anna was moved by a strange tender urge to brush it away.

Leah had taken the golden lenses out, revealing eyes of naked hazel. That gaze had not changed over the years: still so guarded, so watchful and remote.

Anna smiled tiredly. *Look at her*, she thought. *She looks just like me*.

On impulse, she placed a finger to her lips. *Shhh*. Leah's scowl deepened, and the hand at Alan's back tensed into a fist, bunching

126

the T-shirt. Quickly, before he could turn, Anna pushed open the door and stepped out onto the landing.

Closing the door on Leah and Alan, she severed with only the smallest tearing pain the thin membrane that still stretched between herself and them.

Walking down the fire-escape and away, she had not dared to look over her shoulder. But now a strange scraping, rattling sound made her turn: on the opposite pavement, the little girl with skinny plaits was coming down the slope on her roller-blades, frowning in concentration, arms out for balance. She glanced briefly at Anna, and flicked a hand in a brief, ambiguous wave. Then she swung herself around a lamppost and sped away.

In the silence Anna could hear the surf. She felt jittery, startled, hopeful. The sunlight was pale but friendly, and she breathed it in carefully, like some new kind of air.

She turned to face the sea. Today it did not seem wet, or deep; it shimmered in the bright morning light like fragments of peacock feather or insect wing, like something she could reach out and touch with a finger.

Sink or swim.

Starting down the hill, she began to see things in the water: shadows moving, slow and fast, winged, finned, silver and blue; shapes familiar and strange as dreams. And then she was running, the gradient pulling her faster and faster, flying; down towards the railway tracks, the sea, the glittering day.

Acknowledgements

I am deeply grateful to John Coetzee, without whose guidance and help this book could not have been written.

I owe a great deal to the University of Cape Town Creative Writing Masters Course, in which I was enrolled from the beginning of 1997 to mid-1999, and which resulted in the initial manuscript of *Shark's Egg*. Thank you to Lesley Marx and Stephen Watson for their assistance during this time, and to Leon de Kock for his constructive criticism.

I am indebted to the Baird Foundation and the CSD (now the National Research Foundation) for financial support during 1998.

Thank you to Annari van der Merwe at Kwela, for her faith in me; and to Julie-Anne Justus for her meticulous editing. Thanks also to Tony Morphet for his valuable advice and criticism.

I am also grateful to Phil Hockey for identifying the swifts, John Rogers for explaining the rocks, Andrew Putter for his enthusiastic dissection of the plot, and Megan Tjasink for the fishy pictures.

Special love and gratitude go to:
Olivia Rose-Innes, Andrew Rose-Innes, Jeremy Collins, Grant Jardine, Stacey Riley, Margot Schrire and Justin Youens, for – among many, many other things – reading and criticising the manuscript at various stages; Daisy Jones, for getting me to sit down and do it in the first place; faithful ex-housemates Aska Wierzycka and Iain North, for tea and patience; Karen Briner, Darrel Bristow-Bovey, Susie Cowen, Eddie Edwards, Martin Epstein, Charl Hattingh, Evan Milton and Tanya Wilson, for your friendship and support during the writing of this book; and Fremount, for being such a fine creature.